"If I didn't know better, Ann, I'd swear you were hitting on me."

"Hitting on you!" She must have turned six shades of red. "We both agreed to keep it strictly business between us."

"Yeah, that was our agreement," Mike said. "But I'll warn you now, lady, when this business is cleared up, I'll be coming after you."

She stopped and turned around. "What do you mean?"

"We've got a lot of lost pleasure to make up."

"Do you actually think I'm stupid enough to get involved with a guy who lives on the edge like you do?"

"I think it's out of both our hands. Right now I want to pick you up and carry you to bed. Are you really going to deny you don't want me to? No, sweetheart, it won't fly. Those violet eyes tell me all I have to know. And I figure it's going to be worth the wait."

Dear Reader,

Welcome to another month of excitingly romantic reading from Silhouette Intimate Moments. Ruth Langan starts things off with a bang in *Vendetta,* the third of her four DEVIL'S COVE titles. Blair Colby came back to town looking for a quiet summer. Instead he found danger, mystery—and love.

Fans of Sara Orwig's STALLION PASS miniseries will be glad to see it continued in *Bring On The Night,* part of STALLION PASS: TEXAS KNIGHTS, also a fixture in Silhouette Desire. Mix one tough agent, the ex-wife he's never forgotten and the son he never knew existed, and you have a recipe for high emotion. Whether you experienced our FAMILY SECRETS continuity or are new to it now, you won't want to miss our six FAMILY SECRETS: THE NEXT GENERATION titles, starting with Jenna Mills' *A Cry In The Dark.* Ana Leigh's *Face of Deception* is the first of her BISHOP'S HEROES stories, and your heart will beat faster with every step of Mike Bishop's mission to rescue Ann Hamilton and her adopted son from danger. Are you a fan of the paranormal? Don't miss *One Eye Open,* popular author Karen Whiddon's first book for the line, which features a shape-shifting heroine and a hero who's all man. Finally, go *To The Limit* with new author Virginia Kelly, who really knows how to write heart-pounding romantic adventure.

And come back next month, for more of the best and most exciting romance reading around, right here in Silhouette Intimate Moments.

Yours,

Leslie J. Wainger
Executive Editor

Please address questions and book requests to:
Silhouette Reader Service
U.S.: 3010 Walden Ave., P.O. Box 1325, Buffalo, NY 14269
Canadian: P.O. Box 609, Fort Erie, Ont. L2A 5X3

ANA LEIGH
Face of Deception

Silhouette®

INTIMATE MOMENTS™

Published by Silhouette Books

America's Publisher of Contemporary Romance

SILHOUETTE BOOKS

ISBN 0-373-27370-3

FACE OF DECEPTION

Books by Ana Leigh

Silhouette Intimate Moments

The Law and Lady Justice #1230
*Face of Deception #1300

*Bishop's Heroes

ANA LEIGH

Ana Leigh is a Wisconsin native with three children and five grandchildren. From the time of the publication of her first novel in 1981, Ana successfully juggled her time between her chosen career and her hobby of writing, until she officially retired in September 1994 to devote more time to her "hobby." In the past she has been a theater cashier (who married the boss), the head of an accounting department, a corporate officer and the only female on the board of directors of an engineering firm.

This bestselling author received a *Romantic Times* Career Achievement Award nomination for Storyteller of the Year in 1991, the BOOKRAK 1995-1996 Best Selling Author Award, the *Romantic Times* 1995-1996 Career Achievement Award and the *Romantic Times* 1996–1997 Career Achievement Award for Historical Storyteller of the Year. Her novels have been distributed worldwide, including Africa, China and Russia.

To Dave,
The best "Ready Reference"
a mother or author could hope for.

Chapter 1

French Guiana

The SUV sped along the crude road sending a trail of dust into the air—a trail that could easily be observed by anyone in pursuit.

Ann Hamilton shoved back the strands of long hair that had fallen across her eyes and nervously glanced up into the rearview mirror. *Thank God!* I'm not being followed.

She cast a quick look at the curled-up figure asleep on the seat next to her, then returned her attention to the road ahead.

Her heart was aching, and a steady stream of tears made seeing difficult: before driving beyond broadcasting range she'd heard an announcement on the car radio that Clayton Burroughs, British-born official with the European Space Consortium, had been killed by an unknown assassin in Kourou.

Clayton knew he was in danger. That's why he sent us away.

She swiped at her tears and returned her attention to the road.

A dozen questions flashed through her mind in rapid succession. Why did Clayton insist she and Brandon come all the way up to his retreat near the coast to wait for help? If he knew he was in danger, why didn't he come with them? Why hadn't he sought help from the British or American Embassies?

She couldn't believe the man she'd loved as a father was dead. Who would want to kill her beloved Clayton? Could the news report have been mistaken? Now, out of broadcasting range, she had no idea of the latest developments.

Dust and tears painted mucky streaks on her face. Ann brushed them aside just as the car hit a pothole and flew above the ground for several seconds before the wheels bounced back on the road.

Brandon awoke and rubbed his eyes with a balled fist. Raising his towhead, he looked around. "Are we almost there, Ann?"

"Almost, honey. Go back to sleep. I'll wake you when we arrive."

His young forehead creased in a frown and he sat up in the seat. "Are you crying?" When she didn't answer, he asked, "You're crying because Grandfather didn't come with us, aren't you?"

Ann bit down on her lip to force back her sobs. The attempt failed; her tears continued to flow.

At the sight of her misery, Brandon's eyes welled with his own unshed tears. "Please don't cry, Ann."

The youngster's parents had been killed in an airplane crash two years earlier. Now she would have to tell him the devastating news of his grandfather's death. "We've got to try to be very brave, honey," she managed to murmur.

As they sped over the precipitous road, Ann was gripped by panic for their safety, and despair at the thought of Clayton being dead. One question leaped continually to her mind: Why was he killed?

The bordering jungle soon engulfed the road. With only the beams of the car to cut a dim swath of light through the inky blackness, Ann eased up on the accelerator and cut her speed to almost a crawl. Nearing midnight, she halted in front of a small villa.

She jumped out of the car and yanked on a bell that hung at the gate of the tall wall surrounding the courtyard of the secluded house. As Ann waited impatiently, she cast a glance back to Brandon. He looked so small and forlorn, his round, blue eyes were wide with apprehension as they followed her every move.

Tugging impatiently at the bell cord, Ann was relieved to see a light materialize in the house. The caretakers, a local couple named Guillaume and Marie Sellier appeared at the door. The man peered through the darkness to identify whomever had awakened them at such a late hour. Recognizing Ann, he hurried to open the gate as Ann lifted Brandon out of the SUV.

After a perfunctory greeting, Guillaume looked about expectantly. "The *monsieur* did not accompany you, Mademoiselle Hamilton?"

Since the remote area was devoid of telephones and radio, Ann knew the couple would not have heard of Clayton's death.

"Mister Burroughs will not be coming," she said, fighting back her tears. Dear God! How can I explain this to them when I don't understand any of it myself?

"Marie, will you make Brandon a sandwich and a glass of milk? He hasn't eaten anything since morning."

"And you, *mademoiselle?*"

"Nothing for me. I'm not hungry."

When the woman departed with Brandon in tow, Ann sank down on the couch and buried her head in her hands. Her long blond hair draped in a silky curtain about her face—a symbol of the isolated despair she was feeling.

What should I do? Clayton told me to wait here for help. Should I try to get a message to the American Embassy?

She leaned back and closed her eyes. If only it would end by just waking.

"Mademoiselle." Ann felt a gentle nudge on her shoulder and opened her eyes. "I have your tea, *mademoiselle.*"

As if in a trance, Ann thanked the woman and accepted the offering. "Is Brandon in bed?"

"Oui, mademoiselle. The young one waits for you to come to say the good night."

After a few sips of the hot tea, Ann rose wearily to her feet. Until this moment she hadn't realized how exhausted she was. She patted Marie's shoulder. "*Merci,* Marie. I'm sorry to have disturbed you and Guillaume at this late hour. Go to bed now. We won't need anything else tonight." The woman nodded and immediately disappeared.

Pausing outside of Brandon's bedroom, Ann drew a deep breath and grasped the doorknob. Brandon sat in bed playing with a silver coin.

She'd fallen in love with the youngster from the first day the orphaned child had come to live with his grandfather. Brandon felt the same way about her, and followed her around as though she were the mother he had lost.

"So, what have you got there, sport?" she asked, gathering him into her arms.

"Grandfather gave this to me before we left. He said I should keep this coin to remember him by." Intensity registered on his young face. "Why did he say that, Ann?"

Hugging the boy tighter, Ann forced back her tears. She

couldn't lie to him. "Honey, I have something very sad to tell you. Your grandfather...died this morning."

The words sounded so final, as if by voicing the truth the appalling act became a reality.

Brandon remained silent. Ann was uncertain he had understood her until the youngster asked sadly, "Is Grandfather in Heaven now with Mommy and Daddy?"

"Yes, he is, sweetheart." No why or how—just acceptance. She wished he would cry instead of sitting there looking so vulnerable. Her chest knotted with pain at the pathetic sight of the six-year-old child already conditioned to death.

Brushing back the light hair from his forehead, she pressed a kiss to his brow. "Would you like me to stay with you tonight?"

"No. I can stay alone, Ann. I'm a big boy. Grandfather said so."

The brave but tragic announcement wrenched at her heart. She felt tears welling in her eyes. Rising to her feet, she tucked the sheet around him and then leaned over and kissed his cheek. "Go to sleep now, honey. We'll talk about this tomorrow."

"You go to sleep, too. And don't cry, Ann. Grandfather's happy now. He always told me how much he missed my daddy."

As she was about to close the door, Ann saw Brandon open his fist and stare at the coin clutched in his hand. Tears trickled down his cheeks.

"I'll remember you, Grandfather. I promise," he declared fervently. Then he tucked the coin into his pajama pocket.

No longer able to contain her sadness Ann hurried down the hallway to the privacy of her bedroom.

By rote, she went through the motions of preparing herself for bed and was about to retire when the door flung open with such force that it slammed against the wall. A scream burst past her lips at the sight of a man in the doorway waving a weapon at her.

"Out. Out," he ordered sharply, gesturing wildly with the rifle.

"Ann! Ann! Help me," Brandon cried out from the other room.

"Oh, dear God! Brandon!" In her hurry to reach the frightened child, Ann ignored the armed man and rushed past him. Another abductor was pulling the protesting child by the arm out of his bedroom into the living room.

"Take your hands off him," she cried, rushing to Brandon's defense. His captor shoved her away and she fell back onto the couch.

"Don't you hurt her." Brandon's lower lip jutted out pugnaciously as he pounded the chest of his captor. He was sent sprawling next to Ann. She clutched him tightly as they huddled, terrified, while the two servants were herded into the room by more armed men. After a quick exchange, the abductors bound and gagged the servants and took them back to their room.

Several others went into her bedroom, and Ann could hear them ransacking it.

"Up. Up," her captor ordered when they returned. His knowledge of English may have been limited, but his body language and the menacing gestures spoke an international language that was not difficult to interpret as he herded Ann and Brandon into her bedroom.

As frightened as she was, Ann refused to cower under their intimidating glares. "What is the meaning of this? What do you want from us?"

"No talk. You no talk," he barked, and stormed out of the room, slamming the door behind him.

She couldn't believe the devastation their captors had created in such a short time. The room had been thoroughly sacked in their search for weapons and valuables. Bureau drawers had been pulled out and the contents strewn everywhere. Chairs were upended and pictures yanked off the walls.

After Brandon helped Ann put the mattress back on the bed and restore the bedding to a proper order she insisted he go to bed.

"I'm scared, Ann. I don't want to go to sleep. When are these mean men going away?"

"Soon, honey. Soon," she soothed. "Try to sleep. Maybe they'll be gone in the morning."

When he finally settled down, Ann went to the door and tried to hear what the men were saying. From the few fragments of sentences she was able to overhear, she grasped that they were waiting for further instructions before moving Brandon and her to a different location.

Good Lord! Who were these men? Were they responsible for Clayton's death? Were they going to kill her and Brandon, too?

Her breathing came in quick, shallow gasps as her panic mounted. She felt she was choking. Rushing to the window, she raised it and drew several deep breaths. An armed guard outside waved his weapon to indicate she move back inside the room. Irritated, she slammed down the window.

Her nerves were raw, and she could feel herself coming apart. Her fright, Clayton's death and not knowing the reason behind it all had driven her to the brink of losing her control. Brandon's need for her was the only thing keeping her from breaking down.

To occupy herself Ann tidied the room. The task helped to take her mind off her misery until she picked up a framed photograph that had been knocked to the floor. Her eyes misted as she gazed at the cherished face of the distinguished-looking man in his sixties. She had snapped the photograph of Clayton Burroughs the day they met.

''Oh, Clayton.'' Sobbing, she sank in despair to the floor.

Chapter 2

Mike Bishop awoke with a start when Cassidy nudged him with his foot. "I think I just saw the signal."

Saturated with perspiration, he sat up and looked around hastily at the men stretched out on the deck. All were sleeping except for Dave Cassidy at the helm.

Mike pulled out his binoculars and trained the glasses on the shore. The infrared lenses distinguished a ragged coastline capped by a dense jungle. As the boat drew nearer, a light blinked three times from the shore, the pre-arranged signal from the local guide. They were on course.

Frowning, he lowered the glasses, removed a black wool cap and then wiped his brow on the sleeve of his sweater. He ran his fingers through the clipped hair matted to his head and rose to his feet to stretch his cramped muscles. He was hot and sweaty and would have liked to pull off the black sweater that clung to him in wet patches, shuck the pants and boots and dive into the inviting water.

Despite the undulating movement of the small craft, his

step was firm, his back ramrod straight as he crossed the deck.

"We made good time."

Cassidy nodded. "You think the woman and kid are still alive?"

"I'm not psychic! Your guess is as good as mine."

"What's chewing on your ass?" Cassidy asked. "You've been uptight since the briefing."

"Nothing. Nothing's bugging me," Mike growled. He returned to his former seat, picked up a round tin and began smearing black greasepaint on his face. When he was through, only the whites of his eyes could be discerned in the darkness. Passing the tin to Cassidy, he settled back and began to reflect on the mission ahead.

From the quick briefing they'd received from Prince Charming, a British national had been murdered in French Guiana. A contact informed them that the man's six-year-old grandson and American assistant, Ann Hamilton, whom the Agency assigned the code names of Boy Blue and Snow White, had reached a prearranged rescue site, but were now being held prisoners, presumably by those responsible for the Brit's murder. And since his squad was on a training exercise in neighboring Guyana, they were immediately dispatched to go in fast and get the woman and kid. And not make it an international incident. That meant not to take out any of the abductors. What the hell was with the Agency? Did Baker and Waterman think they could just walk through the door and the bastards would hand them the prisoners?

For the dozenth time Bishop reached into his pocket and pulled out the faxed photograph given to him at the briefing. He stared at the woman's face in the picture. Deep-violet eyes veiled with thick dark lashes stared out at him from the photograph. Shoulder-length golden hair feathered in soft curls around a flawless face blessed with a small straight nose and high cheekbones.

Man, she was hot!

He ran his finger absently across her wide, generous mouth. What in hell had been with this Burroughs? The guy had to have known the risks. Only a damn fool would bring a woman along on an assignment.

On second thought, he'd cut the guy some slack. Maybe the poor fool didn't know. Baker had said that Burroughs wasn't actually an agent. That Waterman had asked Burroughs for his help.

Why had Queen Mother asked this Burroughs for help? Espionage was no job for amateurs. So now the poor bastard's dead for his effort.

Mike felt a tightening in his chest. And by this time, the woman and kid are probably dead, too.

When Cassidy began to rouse the men, Mike refolded the paper and returned it to his pocket. He was proud of this team. Known as the Dwarf Squad in the Agency, he, Cassidy, Bolen and Fraser were former Navy SEALs; Williams and Bledsoe had been with the British SAS. Each man was a specialist in a particular field. They had served together as a team for the past three years, and he trusted all of them. Would stake his life on the performance of any one of them. Mike smiled wryly—he'd often had to.

There was nothing to distinguish one of them from the other. They wore no identification. Dressed alike. On this mission, each of them carried an Israeli-made Uzi submachine gun. In addition they all carried a Silver Trident knife, a garrote, grenades and six extra clips of ammo strapped to their waists.

The team never carried survival rations. They survived on whatever the land offered.

The craft touched shore, and they slipped into the water and beached the boat. At the sound of a crackling leaf all six weapons swung toward the man who stepped out of the brush. He identified himself as the contact they were expecting.

"Burroughs's house three *kilomètre*," the man explained, holding up three fingers as he struggled with English. He pointed to a spot on the map that Bishop had extracted from a waterproof packet. "I see nine, maybe ten go into house."

"Did they all have weapons?"

"*Oui.*"

"Automatic weapons?" Mike pursued.

"I not know, *monsieur.*"

"What about servants?"

"Only Guillaume Sellier and his wife."

"Are they friendly?"

"I think yes."

Seeing there was no more information to be gleaned, Mike nodded abruptly. "Williams, Bledsoe, you two have Boy Blue. Bolen and Fraser, the servants. Cassidy and I will take Snow White. Conceal the boat and we'll move out."

Armed with only a machete, their guide slipped silently into the jungle. "Williams, Bledsoe, take the point." The two men followed the man into the forest.

Cassidy came over to him. "Well, we made it this far. Wonder if we've been spotted."

"We'll soon find out," Mike said. He shifted his gaze to the dense foliage surrounding them. Not a leaf stirred. "It's damn quiet."

Cassidy's smile flashed whitely against the greasepaint on his face. "We'll get them out, Mike. I've got good vibes about this mission."

Mike's face slashed into a grim line. "You said that about Beirut, too."

* * *

Mike's heart pounded like a jackhammer. The closer they got to the house, the faster it beat. His hand holding the rifle was clammy and sweaty. He knew he had to get a hold on himself, but he could only think of what they might find when they entered the house. What if the prisoners were dead? He couldn't forget those violet eyes staring at him from that photograph. The time had come to get out of the business; he was losing his objectivity.

Suddenly they were there, no more time for what-ifs. The men halted, awaiting orders. He sent the guide back to his village to protect the man's identity in the event the mission fell apart.

Stay focused, Bishop. Don't lose your objectivity or you'll endanger the squad as well as the woman and kid. He mustn't let his emotions muddy the water. So why in hell was he fighting the urge to run up to the house and burst through the front door?

Mike shook his head to clear his muddled mind and concentrated on the mission. A brick wall surrounded the house. *A damn brick wall!* Bad enough he was battling mental obstacles, now he was confronted by a physical one—a damn brick wall! They could be picked off like sitting ducks as they tried to scale it.

The squad remained concealed as Williams and Bledsoe checked an SUV parked on the outside of the gate. Before moving on, Bledsoe shook his head and indicated with a hand signal that the keys weren't in the ignition.

As Mike passed the car, he glanced inside. A white flowered scarf shimmered like a silky pool on the front seat. He picked it up and brought the material to his nose. The sensuous fragrance hit like a punch to his gut. The damn scarf smells like Violet Eyes looked in the picture— sensuous and sexy.

Round blotches began to dot the flimsy material. Mike glanced up to discover that it was raining. That was a good sign. Rain would muffle the sound of footsteps. Maybe they were getting a little bit of outside help. He stuffed the scarf under his sweater. The piece of silk adhered seductively to his heated skin.

Bledsoe and Williams returned to report that only one man guarded the front door. In addition, the first stumbling block had been eliminated—the gate had been left ajar; they wouldn't have to scale a wall. One by one the men slipped through the gate until all six members of the squad were inside.

A light glowed from a front window of the house. As the squad huddled in the shrubbery, the front door opened and two men stepped outside carrying automatic weapons. One relieved the guard on duty while the other crossed the patio, passing right by the concealed team. Mike motioned to Bolen and Fraser, and the two men followed the gunman.

He gave Cassidy a signal to take out the guard at the front door and his second in command moved away. Bledsoe and Williams worked their way toward the back of the house to check for any other sentries.

Overcoming the guards proved a simple task, and with the perimeter secured, their objective now was to find the prisoners.

Each of the men moved to a window at the rear or sides of the house. Mike selected the one where Williams had discovered a sentry. Raising the window carefully, he peered into the darkened room and could see a figure in the bed. The light was too faint to distinguish whether it was male or female.

Moving cautiously, he climbed into the room, drew the Trident and crossed the room to the bed. He froze in his tracks when he was close enough to identify the sleeping figure.

He'd found Snow White. Boy Blue was asleep beside her.

Bishop slipped the knife back into his boot and leaned over the woman. The sensuous combination of French perfume and woman drifted up in a seductive titillation. He was tempted to clamp his mouth—instead of his hand—over that wide, generous mouth of hers. Objectivity, hell! He'd been in the jungle too long!

Her eyes popped open in alarm and she struggled to rise, but he forced her back down.

"Quiet. We're here to help you."

Incredulity replaced Ann's initial shock and panic. He sounded American! She peered up at the frightening apparition. The room was too dark to see anything except the faint figure of a man dressed in black. But there was nothing faint about the firm hand clamped over her mouth.

"I'm removing my hand. Don't make a sound. Do you understand?" he whispered.

No doubt remained; that voice was American. She nodded, and couldn't have cried out if she wanted to. She was too numb with shock.

He removed his hand and sat down on the edge of the bed. "Don't be frightened," he whispered. "We'll get you out of here. How many men are there?"

Ann wanted to break out in a chorus of "God Bless America." When she finally found her voice, her heart hammered so loudly in her ears, she couldn't hear what she was saying. "I saw eight of them, but I think there were others."

"Is there anyone else in the house besides you and the kid?"

She nodded. "Two servants. The last time I saw them they were tied up in the rear bedroom." Now that the shock had worn off, once again she could feel hysteria mounting within her.

He must have sensed her rising agitation and tried to relax her. "You're doing fine. Now tell me, were all the men armed?"

"I think so. At least all of the ones I saw. Who are these men? Are they the same ones who murdered Clayton?"

"I'll explain everything later. Just remember, they're dangerous, and won't hesitate to kill you or the kid. Do exactly what I say. Did any of them speak English?"

"Poorly."

"Could you understand anything said?"

The man's clipped questions and reticence were beginning to make her feel as if she were on a witness stand. "I think they're waiting for someone—or some instructions. They said something about moving us to a different location."

"Did they say where? Mention any names?"

At the negative shake of her head, his jaw hardened into a grim line. "Did any of them harm you?"

"No."

A trace of a smile tagged at the corners of his mouth. The glimmer was gone before she realized that it might have been an attempt at smiling.

"Will the kid cry when you wake him?"

"I don't know. I don't think so. But this has been a harrowing experience for him."

Bishop stood up. "Get dressed."

"What about Brandon?"

"Let him sleep for the moment."

By now her vision had adjusted to the darkness, and she saw that the man was tall, at least four inches over six feet. He dwarfed her five feet eight inches. Most men she met didn't.

After collecting her clothing, she cast a prim glance in his direction.

"What?"

"I'd like some privacy, please," she said.

"Lady, this is no time to worry about privacy. Just put the damn clothes on."

"Then turn around, Mr.—"

"Bishop." Disgusted, Bishop pivoted. Ann slipped on a pair of lace panties, pulled the nightgown over her head and replaced it with a bra. Jeans and a shirt followed quickly, and as she buttoned the shirt, she slipped her feet into a pair of sneakers.

"You can turn around now."

His look was one of pure annoyance. "Wake the kid, but don't dress him. Just put shoes on him, and for God's sake, keep him quiet."

She leaned over the bed and shook Brandon gently. "Wake up, honey. We have to go."

Brandon was too drowsy to offer an argument. "Where are we going?"

"These are friends, Brandon. They've come to help us. You must do everything they tell you to do. Do you understand?" She slipped his feet into shoes and tied the laces.

Suddenly a face filled the window. "You all set?"

"Yeah," Bishop said. He moved to the window. "Everyone out?"

The man never stopped scanning the courtyard as he spoke. "All except Williams and Bledsoe, they can't find the boy."

"He's here. Let's move out before bullets start flying."

"Bishop!" Ann whispered, pointing to the door that had just begun to open.

Bishop shoved her and Brandon to the floor behind the bed, and then crouched down on a knee with his weapon pointed at the door. A dark figure slipped cautiously into the room.

Bishop relaxed and rose to his feet. "What in hell are you doing? I almost shot you," he hissed. "Get in here and shut that door."

Another man followed behind and gently eased the door shut.

"All these bloody blokes are sleeping like babies. We've searched this whole house and there's no sign of—"

"He's here," Bishop said. He nodded in the direction of the bed. As if to confirm his words, Brandon peered over the top of the bed, his eyes rounded with excitement.

"Let's move," Bishop ordered.

One of the men lifted Brandon into his arms. "Hey, sonny, how'd you like to go for a walk?"

"Is Ann coming?"

"I sure am, honey," she assured him.

"Let's go, lady," Bishop said, and grabbed her hand.

Once outside, Brandon, Marie and Guillaume were lifted onto the backs of three of them, and they started in a run down the jungle path. A fourth man knelt down on a knee.

"Climb on," Bishop said.

"That won't be necessary. I jog every day," Ann said.

She bore another one of his black glares. "Okay, but if you slow us up, I'll have to carry you."

A hard run through a jungle in a rain was a far different cry from her usual jogging. Ann's lungs felt near to bursting when they stopped and uncovered a concealed boat.

Bishop and one of the men crouched down to guard the rear as Ann lingered, saying goodbye to the two servants who were returning to their village.

"When those gunmen leave, we return to house," Guillaume assured her.

"I'll contact you as soon as I can," Ann said.

"Let's get out of here before someone gets killed," Bishop ordered, his eyes trained on the jungle.

"God be with you," Ann said. Guillaume took his wife's hand, and they disappeared into the jungle.

An hour later, off the coast of French Guiana, Ann smiled up gratefully at the freckle-faced airman, who looked as American as a parade on the Fourth of July, as he reached out a helping hand and assisted her into an unmarked helicopter.

Chapter 3

A single light glowed dimly in the cabin of the helicopter. The squad lay sprawled asleep wherever the men could find room.

Ann felt as if they'd been flying for hours, yet the sun had not risen, so she knew she was mistaken. She raised her arm to check the time and realized she wasn't wearing a watch. She had fled Kourou so hurriedly that morning she'd forgotten to put it on.

The whole series of events remained a mystery to Ann. Clayton's death. The men who tried to abduct her. These men. Where were they taking Brandon and her? They all seemed friendly enough except for their uptight leader. At least she knew their names now, but nothing more.

Dazed, she leaned back against the cabin wall and closed her eyes. How did she lose control of her life in such a short span of time? She was fleeing South America with only the clothes on her back. No money. Not even a damn watch on her wrist!

Relax, Ann. Try to sleep. But sleep was an impossibility. The chopper's rotors were noisy, the vibration jerked the craft, the floor was hard and her legs were cramped.

Lord, how I hate helicopters! What am I doing in this crate flying over the Atlantic...that is, if we are over the Atlantic.

She hugged Brandon tighter against her, readjusting his sleeping head in her lap. His nearness was a warm and gratifying reassurance that she had not lost her sanity.

She suddenly felt a prickly sensation and knew she was being watched. Glancing up, she discovered Bishop staring at her under hooded lids. For a brief moment their gazes locked. His expression remained unchanged, and she blushed before shifting her eyes downward.

She wondered what such a man thought about in quiet moments like this. The next mission? A woman? Fearing his enigmatic eyes could read her mind, Ann closed her eyes.

She continued to feel his intense stare.

Ann awoke to discover the chopper was landing. All the men were awake and alert. From her position on the floor, she couldn't see anything until the freckle-faced crewman opened the door as they touched down. Then the glare of bright sunlight hit her in the eyes.

Two of the men jumped out with pointed rifles, then Bishop got out and swung her to the ground. The other two followed with Brandon.

Bishop took her by the arm while Cassidy moved to her side and put a hand on her elbow, as well. They whisked her toward an unmarked plane standing nearby on the runway. She felt like a prisoner being hustled away to jail.

Curious, she glanced around but all that she saw was a deserted airstrip. No hangars. No tower. Nothing. She couldn't venture a guess as to their location.

Was it possible these men, in fact, were the ones responsible for Clayton's death? Maybe the men at the villa merely intended to abduct Brandon and her for ransom.

Ann felt certain about one thing: the long-on-silence, short-on-explanation Bishop was not about to volunteer any information.

Brandon's boyish laughter penetrated her rumination. Ann turned her head to look back and saw that the one named Bledsoe was carrying the youngster on his shoulders. Thank God there's a spark of humanity in at least one of these men.

Immediately she regretted her callous attitude. She was foolish and ungrateful, allowing her imagination to run rampant. These men had risked their lives to save her and Brandon.

Under a blush of guilt, she stole a glance at the sculpted profile of Bishop, who was walking beside her. Now that he had wiped off the greasepaint, the man appeared to be in his mid-thirties. His nose had clearly been broken at least once, and tiny lines crept from the corners of his eyes; but these features tended to add character to his face, she reflected with the objective eye of a photographer. A thick mustache nestled above a firm mouth with a sensual lower lip. Seasoned by sun and wind, this was not a handsome face by Hollywood standards—no Brad Pitt or Antonio Banderas for sure. No, indeed. But she was willing to stake her professional reputation that women who had gazed into those melancholy, deep-hazel eyes of his had found the face sensuously irresistible.

Daring to intrude on the thoughts of her taciturn guard, Ann said boldly, "I'd like to know where we're going, Bishop."

"You'll find out when the time comes." That earlier, welcome-sounding American voice now had a decided growl of irritation. But its huskiness, coupled with those bedroom eyes of his, could still play havoc with a girl's libido.

For heaven's sake, Ann, there hasn't been time enough for you to have developed Stockholm Syndrome!

She had had enough of the whole scene and stopped abruptly, shrugged off their hands and with flashing eyes squared off against the two men.

"I don't want to appear ungrateful for what you've done for Brandon and me, but I've tolerated all the pushing and shoving I intend to. Until I start getting some answers from you wardens…watchdogs…or whatever, I'm not going to budge another step." She folded her arms across her chest to reinforce the declaration.

The party following halted, shuffling impatiently as they looked to their leader. Without saying a word, Bishop swept her up in his arms, carried her onto the plane and then dumped her into what appeared to be a seat.

"Be sure and fasten your seat belt, lady."

The smug gleam in his hazel eyes taunted her to go for his jugular. However, her dignity prevailed. Instead she bestowed a scathing glower upon him. "Do you have an aversion to heights, Bishop?"

"Why do you ask?"

"You seem to prefer airplanes without windows. Or haven't you noticed there are no windows in this plane, either?"

"We've been told that after this trip we'll have earned enough frequent-flyer points to rate one that does."

His sarcasm was exasperating. "What kind of plane is this, Bishop?"

"You writing a book?"

"An exposé. I'll be sure to spell your name correctly." He didn't even blink. "It's a C-17."

"C as in cargo?"

"You've got that right."

"Is it privately owned, or does it belong to the United States? There are no markings on it."

"I hadn't noticed," he said.

He was a very exasperating man. To her further chagrin he sat down beside her.

Determined to ignore him, Ann turned away. An awkward silence developed as they marked time while the others got situated. Brandon was put in a jump seat directly across the aisle from hers. She watched Bledsoe tighten the boy's seat belt, then pretend to tickle him.

The sound of Brandon's irrepressible laughter brought a tender smile to Ann's lips. "Your friend seems to like children."

He glanced at Bledsoe and shrugged negligently in reply. Ann decided to remain civilized, no matter how much this man irritated her.

"Do you like children, Bishop? Ah, do you have a first name or is Bishop a clerical title?" She thought it was a clever remark. His expression never changed.

"Bishop will do," he said.

"Do you like children, Bishop?"

A brow quirked. "Never thought about it one way or another."

Their conversation ceased when the plane started to roll down the runway, and she waited until they were airborne to pose her next remark.

"I think Brandon and I should be sitting together."

He fixed a condescending gaze on her. "We have a reason for everything we do, Hamilton."

"Who is 'we,' Bishop?"

"You'll get your answers when we land."

This time he grinned. Ann figured if she hadn't been sitting, the devastating shock would have knocked her off her feet.

"Why don't you try to rest?" His crooked smile was

engaging. She quickly turned her head away from the appealing sight. The Stockholm Syndrome wasn't going to work on her.

Shifting to her side, she leaned her head against the windowless cabin wall of the C-17 and closed her eyes.

Mike watched her as she slept. For damn sure she was a knockout beauty. Looking at her and breathing in that perfume she wore conjured up an image of tropical nights, soft music, the smell of jasmine drifting in from outside—and the two of them in bed making out all night long.

She sure had more going for her than just a pretty face. He'd seen the spark in her violet eyes when she had challenged him, and he liked that. It was a sign she was a survivor. The woman had taken a couple of knockout punches in the last twenty-four hours and appeared to be climbing back up on her feet. Yeah, there was more to Ann Hamilton than just the damnedest pair of eyes he'd ever seen.

Ann woke up in darkness. They were landing but she had no idea how long she'd been asleep or where they were. She felt the touchdown, and then the plane taxied for several minutes before coming to a halt. When the door opened, the light was almost blinding. She shaded her eyes to avoid the glare, and by the time her eyesight adjusted, Bishop and his crew had transferred them into another helicopter. The copter's rotors were already revolving and within seconds they had lifted off.

This one was larger than the previous one, and had actual seats. She was grateful for that, because her aching body was feeling the effects from the two previous uncomfortable means of transportation.

But where were they, and where were they going now? She reached to shove aside a curtain that shrouded the windows. Immediately a firm hand clamped over her wrist.

"Give it a couple more minutes, Hamilton."

Ann turned around in disgust. He was leaning across her, their faces inches apart. She sucked in a gasp, and the hazel eyes shifted to her parted lips. For a breathless moment she waited, speechless, then he released her wrist and settled back in his seat

"As much as I hate helicopters, I have to say this one is more comfortable than any I've ever been in before. What kind is it?"

"What in hell difference does it make to you?"

"Chapter Two. Have you forgotten?"

Annoyed, he shook his head. "It's a H-53 Sea Stallion. So now you know. Does that clear it all up for you?"

"No, but I'm impressed. It has windows! Can I peek now?"

He leaned over her again, and she breathed in the husky male scent of him as he shoved aside the curtain to reveal a huge window that offered a panoramic view. The lights below appeared as plentiful as the stars above, but it was too dark and they were traveling too swiftly to distinguish any landmarks below.

Suddenly her heart seemed to leap to her throat as she gasped with joy. Ablaze with light, the alabaster beauty of the Washington Monument pierced the darkness like a shining beacon.

They were in Washington, D.C., United States of America.

Ann turned to Bishop and smiled through the tears of joy that streaked her cheeks.

She couldn't believe it when the helicopter landed on the top of a building. But before she could even comment on it, they were rushed into an elevator and then hurried outside to three parked limos. Cassidy hustled Ann into the back seat of the middle car and then sat down next to the driver. Bolen and Fraser moved to the lead vehicle.

Ann looked out the back window in time to see Williams and Bledsoe thrust Brandon into the last car. Before she could protest this latest separation from Brandon, Bishop climbed in beside her and slammed the door.

''We're rolling,'' he mouthed into the radio clutched in his left hand. The limo shot forward with the smooth glide of an Olympic skater.

''What now, Bishop?'' Ann's feeling of complacency at being back in the States was becoming eclipsed quickly by the continued security measures.

''Debriefing.''

''Debriefing? Is that where you strap on the electrodes or shoot me full of sodium pentothal?''

She perceived the barest glimmer of a smile—or was it a smirk? Bishop turned his head and stared out the window.

The conversation had ended, but her awareness of the man beside her increased as the male essence of him continued to tantalize her senses as much as his autocracy provoked them.

Chapter 4

Purring like a contented black cat on a velvet cushion, the limo continued to move swiftly on the beltway. After a short ride, they passed through a gate with an armed guard and pulled up at the rear of a building.

Ann and Brandon were whisked up several floors in an elevator and led to an office. Bishop rapped lightly, opened the door and peered inside. Satisfied, he stepped aside for Ann and Brandon to enter and then followed them into the room. As irritating as the man could be, she felt relieved to have his commanding presence beside her.

The two men awaiting their arrival rose to their feet, and one stepped forward to greet her.

"Miss Hamilton, I'm Avery Waterman. I can't tell you how relieved we are to see you've arrived safely."

His clipped accent was clearly British. He appeared to be in his late fifties or early sixties. Everything about Waterman mirrored refined elegance, from a well-groomed mustache to the European cut of the charcoal-colored cashmere jacket tailored to fit his slim figure.

Waterman shook Ann's hand, then leaned over and patted Brandon on the head. "And this chap must be our young Mr. Burroughs."

The move was too aggressive for the confused six-year-old. He slipped his hand into Ann's. She grasped it securely.

Waterman did not miss the gesture. He straightened up, and his gray eyes focused on Ann. "Please be seated, Miss Hamilton. May I introduce my associate, Jeffrey Baker?"

Baker nodded his head of salt-and-pepper hair closely cropped in a buzz cut. "Miss Hamilton." The deep guttural greeting seemed to be dredged from the abyss of his barrel chest.

She observed that Baker appeared to be the antithesis of his colleague. Shorter than Waterman by several inches, Baker resembled a retired Marine gunny sergeant. Missing were the familiar string of hash marks running up his sleeve, or rows of combat ribbons lining his chest, but she was convinced the inscription Semper Fi was probably tattooed somewhere on the solid brawn concealed beneath his wrinkled, gray flannel suit.

Ann sat down on a nearby couch. When Brandon curled against her side, Waterman addressed the youngster. "Brandon, would you like something to eat?"

Brandon looked to Ann for approval. He grinned broadly when she nodded. Bishop led the boy to the door, and for several moments carried on a whispered conversation with the men in the hallway. Two of them departed with Brandon in tow.

"I hope I'm finally going to get some answers," Ann declared after Bishop returned, crossed his arms and leaned against the wall.

Avery Waterman sat down opposite Ann and settled back with a condescending smile. "Ask away, Miss Hamilton. We're at your service."

Yeah, right! She resented the cat-and-mouse game still being played. Within the past thirty some hours Clayton had been murdered, she and Brandon terrorized and virtually spirited out of South America. Now this man had the audacity to patronize her.

"Mr. Waterman, just who are you and whom do you represent?"

She didn't fail to catch the hasty glance that Waterman exchanged with his associate. "I assure you, Miss Hamilton, you are in good hands."

"That's not what I asked, Mr. Waterman."

"We are an antiterrorist rescue division, Miss Hamilton."

"Of what? British Intelligence or the CIA?"

His mouth curled in a slight smile. "CIA, Miss Hamilton."

"Do you know who killed Clayton Burroughs?"

"Not as yet. We were hoping you could tell us."

Startled by the unexpected voice at her side, as much as by the astonishing remark, Ann turned her head to discover Jeffrey Baker had crossed the room and was now standing next to the couch. She had been unaware he had moved closer, for despite his bull-like physique, the man had moved quickly and quietly.

"Me? How would I know?" she asked, flabbergasted.

Waterman leaned forward. "Miss Hamilton, we are aware of your close association with Mr. Burroughs."

"Close association? What do you... Clayton and I were close friends...nothing more..." Ann floundered helplessly. She took a deep breath. Why was she allowing these men to put her on the defensive? To intimidate her? Their implications smeared a beautiful friendship.

"I didn't mean to imply otherwise, Miss Hamilton," Waterman added hastily. "But we also know you were seen with Burroughs the morning he was killed. Did he say anything that would offer a clue as to the identity of his assailants?''

Ann shook her head. ''No. Nothing. He never mentioned he was in danger.''

''Think carefully, Miss Hamilton. Tell us exactly what transpired yesterday morning. Don't spare the minutest detail.'' His tone had lost its loftiness, and his clear gray eyes were bathed in kindness.

Ann allowed her mind to drift back to the dreadful morning. ''Clayton telephoned me early and said the situation was urgent. I had never heard him sound so grave. He told me to pack an overnight bag and come over at once.''

Ann closed her eyes, recalling the desperation in Clayton's voice. ''When I arrived at his home, he shoved Brandon into his car and told me to drive to his villa in the north. He would join us there later.'' She lifted her hands in despair. ''That's all I know.''

''He said nothing more to you?''

''Oh, there was one other thing.'' Both men leaned forward attentively. ''He said, 'I know you'll take good care of Brandon.'''

''He offered no explanation? And you didn't ask for one?'' Waterman asked skeptically.

''No. Everything happened so fast I just reacted automatically without questioning his motives. Why didn't he come with us?''

''I suspect he knew whomever was found with him would be killed, too,'' Baker said.

Tears began to streak her cheeks. ''I feel as if I deserted him…abandoned him. If only I had known he was in danger.''

Waterman patted her hand. ''There's nothing you could have done to prevent what happened.''

She jerked up her head and glared at him. "I could have called the police. They would have protected him."

"Who knows, Miss Hamilton, the police may be the very ones responsible for his death."

"You're wrong," she lashed out. "French Guiana is a beautiful country—a Shangri-la. There is no corruption there. The people there have an innocence like none other I've seen anywhere."

Waterman stood up. "Well, apparently not all are innocent. Mr. Burroughs's death testified to that."

"Clayton was not killed by one of the local citizens," she declared adamantly. "You must have some idea why he was murdered. The CIA wouldn't have gone to all the trouble of bringing me here if you thought his death was just a…random killing."

Waterman moved away and sat down behind a desk. "Miss Hamilton, I must have your promise that whatever I tell you will not go beyond this room." Ann nodded. "As Burroughs's aide you must have been familiar with the satellite the Israeli government intended to launch."

"I assume you're referring to the launch aborted last month because of a mechanical malfunction."

Baker nodded. "But there was no mechanical malfunction. We have reason to suspect the satellite had been sabotaged. Burroughs was conducting an undercover investigation in an attempt to find out who was behind that destruction."

Sabotage! Undercover investigation! Ann could not believe what she heard. "Are you saying Clayton was an agent…with the CIA?"

"Let's say that Mr. Burroughs was engaged in undercover work for the government, but he was neither a trained agent nor an employee of the Central Intelligence Agency. He contacted us because of his suspicions."

Ann shook her head to try and clear her befuddled

thoughts. "Why would he contact the United States? The satellite was Israeli. Why wouldn't he contact the Israeli government? It was their problem, not the United States'."

"Whatever he was pursuing was linked to the United States. He had found out that much."

"And died because of it," Ann said bitterly. "Clayton Burroughs was the kindest, gentlest man I've ever known. How dare you encourage him in this investigation?" Appalled, her voice rose to near hysteria. "If what you say is true, why didn't you let your own operators investigate this…sabotage?" She glared at Bishop, who had not said a word throughout the whole conversation. "Lord knows you've got enough of them."

Cradling her head in her hand, she refused to give in to further tears. Particularly with three sets of eyes watching her every move.

"You're tired now, Miss Hamilton," Waterman said. "This has been a terrible strain on you. I think you should get some rest."

Ann lifted her head. "Your Mr. Bishop rushed us away so hurriedly that I don't have any money, not even a change of clothing. And, as you saw, Brandon is in his pajamas."

Waterman's smile bordered on a simper. "Agent Bishop's propensity for expediency is what makes him so effective in the field." He assisted her to her feet, put a hand on her back and steered her toward the door. "We'll see that you get whatever you need. And we've made arrangements for you at the Watergate."

Ann stopped at the doorway. "What about Clayton's body?"

"The British government is handling the arrangements. Mr. Burroughs's remains will be returned to England for burial."

"I would like to attend the funeral and then return to Kourou as quickly as possible. Everything I own is there."

"Of course, Miss Hamilton. You'll be free to move about as soon as we are certain you'll be safe. The important thing now is for you and the lad to get a good night's rest." The patronizing attitude had returned.

When Bishop opened the door, Ann saw Brandon curled up asleep in a chair. Her gaze sought Bishop and locked with that of the hazel-eyed squad leader.

"Agent Bishop, come in here a moment," Baker called to him.

Mike Bishop broke their fixed stare and stepped back inside. As the door was closing, Ann heard Baker say, "The woman's no fool. Do you think she's telling us everything she knows?"

The door clicked shut before Ann could hear Waterman's reply. She glanced at Cassidy and offered a nervous smile.

Cassidy grinned and winked in understanding.

Within minutes Bishop rejoined them. Cassidy picked up Brandon and they headed for the elevator.

"We're moving," Bishop said into the radio clutched in his hand. The voices of Bolen, then Williams, acknowledged the message through the transmitter.

"I thought you agents talked into your lapels," she joked lightly.

"Not since I sent my suit to the cleaners," Bishop replied.

"Bishop, you actually made a joke!"

Bolen and Fraser were waiting when the elevator doors opened.

"Tell me, Bishop, are we all checking into the hotel together?" Ann asked when they stepped outside, and Bledsoe and Williams joined them. "I'm beginning to feel like Snow White.'' The six men exchanged startled glances.

''Only thing is one of the seven dwarfs appears to be missing. Which one of the little darlings are you, Bishop— Grumpy or Dopey?''

Bishop's face hardened into a grim frown. ''Did anyone ever tell you, Hamilton, what a pain in the ass you are?''

''Oh, lighten up, Bishop, I was only joking.''

Yeah, she was right, he had to lighten up, Mike told himself. But Violet Eyes was unaware of how close her quip had hit home. Or maybe she did. Maybe she knew more than she was admitting. Maybe she knew why Tony Sardino, the seventh member of the Dwarf Squad—code name Bashful—had been killed the month before in Beirut.

Chapter 5

Brandon was still asleep in the other bed when Ann awoke the following morning. She sat up and glanced around the hotel room, her attention drawn immediately to a flight bag on the dresser. The small satchel had not been there when she went to bed.

Bishop must have brought in the bag while I was sleeping. Doesn't he ever sleep?

Dressed only in her underclothes, Ann wrapped the sheet around her and padded barefoot over to examine the bag's contents.

"Bless you, Bishop. I take back every nasty thought I've had of you," she mumbled as she pulled out toothbrushes, toothpaste, a hairbrush, a comb, shampoo, socks, underwear for Brandon and a jogging suit for him, as well. There was even a bottle of her favorite perfume.

Ann stopped momentarily, and her face deepened in a blush when she withdrew the final articles from the bag: a lacy black bra and a matching pair of bikinis.

"Damn you, Bishop," she grumbled, revoking her earlier benediction. "How did you know my size?"

She tossed them aside and eagerly scooped up the toilet articles. Then, frowning, she reconsidered, snatched up the lingerie and disappeared into the bathroom.

After a leisurely shampoo and shower, Ann poked her head out of the bathroom. She cast a fretful glance at her jeans and shirt hanging on the back of a chair across the room. Brandon appeared to be asleep, but dare she chance retrieving her clothes dressed in only a bra and panties? It would just be the time he'd awaken.

He who hesitates is lost, Ann. She dashed across the room and grabbed the garments. When she turned to run back to the bathroom, she stopped abruptly, and the clothes dropped to the floor. Her mouth gaped open in a scream that froze in her throat when she recognized Bishop.

"What…what are you doing here?"

Ann instinctively wanted to cover herself with her hands, but she fought the reflex. After all, she had photographed dozens of lingerie ads, and lingerie revealed less than today's swimsuits.

However, standing in the intimacy of a hotel room, dressed only in a skimpy bra and panties that *he* had bought, somehow did not equate in her mind to the impersonal professionalism of a photo shoot. Especially with Bishop's hazel-eyed gaze fixed on her.

His damn eyes are like the lens of a camera. They don't miss a detail.

Bishop slowly rose to his feet, bent over and picked up her jeans and shirt and then held them out to her. "I see they fit." His eyes glimmered with smugness.

She snatched the garments out of his outstretched hand and pulled on the shirt. "I don't appreciate this intrusion of my privacy, Bishop."

"Only doing my job, Hamilton."

She jerked up her head. "I thought your job involved rescue operations. Do your responsibilities extend to selecting women's lingerie?"

He shrugged his broad shoulders. "A man's gotta do what a man's gotta do." He plopped back down in the chair.

"Funny, Bishop." She moved to the dresser. "How did you know my size?"

"I've got eyes."

That you have, Bishop. Disturbing eyes. She could feel the sweep of them as she worked the jeans past her hips.

Dabbing on a few drops of the Chanel he had brought, Ann asked, "And my favorite perfume?"

"I've got a nose."

"And a big mouth." She grabbed the comb and brush and stormed into the bathroom, slamming the door in frustration.

The noise woke Brandon. The youngster sat up and grinned when he saw Mike. "Hi, Mr. Bishop."

"Morning, kid. Do you always sleep this late?"

"Not always. Just the mornings I don't wake up early."

It was that kind of children's logic that had convinced Mike he'd never make a good father.

Brandon's smile quickly vanished as he glanced around the room. Panic began to flood the boy's features. "Where's Ann?"

"She's in the bathroom. She'll be out in a minute."

Brandon's face puckered and he began to cry. "I want Ann. Where is she?"

Hearing Brandon's cry, Ann hurried out of the bathroom and rushed over to gather him into her arms. "I'm right here, honey." She glared accusingly at Bishop. "What did you say to upset him?"

Mike moved to the door and opened it. "Get the kid dressed, Hamilton. We're due back at the Agency."

*   *   *

Baker and Waterman were waiting in the same room, in the same positions as the day before. Only their clothing had changed. Waterman was now wearing a dark-gray, three-piece suit that didn't have a wrinkle; Baker had on a brown suit that looked as if he had put it on before going to bed last night.

This time she had a strategy. Before either man could try any of their intimidating tactics on her, Ann took the offensive.

"Gentlemen, how much longer must Brandon and I endure these stringent security measures?"

Waterman offered an ingratiating smile. "We understand, Miss Hamilton. My associate and I have conferred on this matter and have reached the decision that any threat to you was left behind in French Guiana."

She felt a sense of relief until hit by a sudden thought. "Are you suggesting I not return to that country?"

Baker nodded. "Not at this time. I certainly wouldn't advise you to do so until we clear up the mystery behind Mr. Burroughs's death."

"But everything I own…"

Cutting off her protest, he handed her an envelope. "We've made whatever arrangements are necessary. Your account has been transferred to a bank here in Washington."

Ann opened the envelope and stared dumbfounded at the contents. It contained her checkbook, credit card and passport. "Where…how did you get these?"

"We have our ways, Miss Hamilton." Baker continued to speak as if by rote, sounding like a police officer reading the Miranda warning to a suspect. "We appreciate your past cooperation and apologize for any inconvenience you may have suffered while under our protection. We only had your interests at heart."

Ann couldn't believe how these arrangements had been made so quickly, but she felt a great burden had been lifted off her shoulders. "Then Brandon and I are free to leave."

Her exhilaration was quickly squelched when the two security heads exchanged a guarded glance. Waterman cleared his throat and began to hedge.

"Well, one minor problem still exists, Miss Hamilton. Legally, Brandon Burroughs is a British subject. Her Majesty's government prefers he remain at their embassy."

She tightened her grasp on Brandon's hand. "I won't hear of it. I'm the only family he has now. He'll be frightened without me."

"It will only be for a few days, Miss Hamilton, while a proper investigation is made to determine if the child has any other living relatives. If not, we are recommending he then be placed in your custody."

"I can tell you right now Clayton Burroughs was Brandon's last remaining relative. His parents were killed in an accident. His mother had been an orphan. Brandon's father had been Clayton's only son. Clayton's wife and daughter were both dead, and Clayton had no siblings. I've seen his will. He's appointed me Brandon's legal guardian."

Waterman offered an indulgent smile. "Then that should simplify the matter, Miss Hamilton. But we still must follow the proper procedures to determine the legality of the situation for ourselves."

"I can't believe with all your apparent…connections, Mr. Waterman, that you can't cut through the red tape and let Brandon remain with me. He's so young. This will be frightening and confusing to him. Hasn't he suffered enough?"

Waterman's expression softened with understanding, while Baker's remained inscrutable. "We tried, Miss Hamilton," Waterman said.

"May I visit him at the Embassy?"

"Every day, if you wish. I shall make the arrangements myself."

She glanced down at Brandon's upturned face. The young boy knew he was being discussed, but he couldn't follow the conversation. "May I have a moment alone with him?"

"Of course."

After the two men left the room, Ann knelt down and smiled as she straightened his collar. "Sweetheart, I guess we've got to split up for a few days."

"No. I don't want to," he declared.

"Neither do I, honey, but since I'm not your real mother, we have to do what these men say."

"We don't have to listen to these dumb guys, Ann. We can run away from them." He started to sob and flung his arms around her neck. "Let's go back to Grandfather's house. I bet Mr. Bishop would help if we asked him."

She hugged him for several moments. "Sweetheart, I promise that we'll be together again as soon as Mr. Waterman can arrange it."

She kissed his cheek and pulled back, smiling at him through her tears. "Now, you're going to have a real good time while you're staying at the British Embassy. I'll come and visit you every day until you can leave with me."

His little chin quivered. "You promise?"

Her heart felt as if it was being ripped from her chest. "Promise."

As Brandon wiped away his tears, Ann rose to her feet and opened the door. She nodded. "He's ready."

Agents Bledsoe and Williams followed the security heads into the room.

"Come on, lad, we'll stop on the way and get us some ice-cream cones," Williams announced.

Brandon's eyes brightened. "Bye, Ann." He grinned up at Bledsoe. "Can I have a chocolate one, Pete?"

"You bet, lad. A two-scooper."

"I'll see you tomorrow, sweetheart," Ann called out as the two Englishmen took the small boy in hand and led him away.

"We'll notify you as soon as the legalities are finalized, Miss Hamilton," Waterman said. "Will you be remaining at the Watergate?"

Ann nodded. "I'll expect to hear from you."

Bishop followed her to the elevator and pushed the down button. "I'll flag you a cab."

"That won't be necessary. I think I'd like to walk for a while."

A bell chimed, the door swung open and Ann stepped into the elevator. She looked up into his troubled gaze. "I want to thank you for everything, Bishop. I'm sorry I snapped at you this morning."

Before he could reply, the door closed and the hazel eyes were gone from sight. She'd miss them.

Ann had never felt so lonely in her life.

Chapter 6

After the relatively arcadian existence she had been living for the past four years, the sights and sounds of metropolitan Washington were a new experience for Ann. She dodged people and traffic for an hour and then entered a mall. To her surprise the shops were not open, but she saw people using the hallways to do their morning walking and jogging. Ann joined them, perusing the shop windows as she passed.

By the time she finished, she had mentally noted several outfits to try on, and sat down to wait for the shops to open. As she listened to the pleasant music in the mall, her thoughts wandered to Brandon and how he was faring. Remembering the earlier conversation, Ann grinned and shook her head. Good heavens! I wonder if they actually did stop for ice cream at this hour of the morning.

Suddenly she felt an uneasy twinge at the nape of her neck—someone was watching her. She looked around. Several of the nearby benches were filled with the joggers and walkers whom she remembered seeing previously. None of them appeared to be paying any attention to her.

Ann turned back, but the uneasy feeling continued to nag her. So much so, she decided to leave and return later. Just as she rose to her feet, the mall began to echo with the rattle and clang of iron grills as the shop owners began to unlock and open their stores. So instead of departing, she went to the ATM machine and got some cash, then headed for a small boutique to make her first purchase. However, she couldn't lose the feeling of being followed.

Once engrossed in shopping, her anxiety was forgotten with the pleasure of picking out several outfits, hosiery, shoes and nightgowns. She even stopped and selected a few pieces of lingerie. "Without your assistance, Bishop," she mumbled in satisfaction.

Ann immediately chastised herself for allowing her thoughts to stray to that overbearing agent when she should have been thinking about Brandon.

To ease her conscience, Ann hurried to the children's department and bought him several pairs of sweatpants and shirts. As she continued to browse through the store, a gold silk blouse caught her fancy.

"Isn't it lovely? It just came in yesterday," the gray-haired saleswoman remarked.

"Yes, I think I'll try it on."

"The dressing room is right back here." The clerk led her to an alcove at the rear of the store and pushed aside the curtain of one of the stalls. "My name is Janice. Just call out if you need any help."

Ann had just removed the blouse and put her shirt back on when the room was plunged into darkness except for a red exit sign over the door. She quickly buttoned her shirt-front and then groped for her packages in the dark.

Suddenly she had an uneasy feeling that she no longer was alone. Someone had entered the darkened room, and

she doubted it was Janice, or the clerk would have identified herself.

Ann felt a sense of peril. Her heart hammered and her
senses attuned sharply to every noise around her. She
heard a soft shuffle of footsteps at the same instant the
distant drone of Janice's voice carried from somewhere
farther out in the store. Whoever was there in the darkness
with her definitely wasn't the sales clerk.

Her nerve ends tingled as footsteps moved stealthily
across the floor. Ann held her breath, but the sound of her
heartbeat pounding in her ears was so loud she felt the
mysterious intruder could hear it as well. Frozen with fear,
she was fearful of moving lest she reveal her whereabouts.

*No, I'm not going to surrender to fear again. Whoever's
following me is in for a surprise. I'm not going down
without a fight.*

She groped for her purse in the dark. It was the only
weapon she had, and as soon as those curtains parted,
she'd swing it at the person's head.

She heard the faint slide of the curtains. He was checking the stalls. *If only he wasn't between her and the door
she'd make a run for it.* But not knowing his exact whereabouts, she might run right into his arms.

*And where the hell was that clerk? She should have
come back to check on her customer. If I get out of here
alive, I'll be damned if I buy that blouse!*

She heard a footstep, this time nearer. Now he couldn't
be more than a few stalls away. She raised her purse in
readiness.

Suddenly a flashlight beam pierced the darkness. "Ann.
Ann, where are you?"

She recognized Bishop's voice at once. "Here. Over
here," she shouted in relief. The light swung in her direction.

She heard his running footsteps, and the drapes before

her parted. With a sob of relief she collapsed against the hard wall of his chest, and his arms closed protectively around her. For several seconds she savored the comfort and strength she felt from the arms enfolding her.

"Let's get out of here." His voice was a husky whisper at her ear. She nodded her response against his chest, and his warm grasp closed around her hand.

Once out of the dressing room, the store was dimly lit by light filtering in from the atrium in the mall. Ann turned to look back at the darkened dressing room. Nothing stirred. She wanted to bolt out of the store, but forced herself to take a deep, calming breath.

"What are you doing here, Bishop?"

"I...ah..."

"So you're the one who's been following me. Damn it, Bishop, you almost scared me to death back there." Anger replaced her former fear. "Why did Mr. Baker lie to me? Lead me to believe it was all over, if he intended to continue playing these cloak-and-dagger games with me?" Her voice cracked. "I was frightened, Bishop. Really frightened."

He didn't offer any word in defense. Instead he took her arm and led her over to a restaurant opposite the shop.

"I haven't been following you, Hamilton," he said, once they were seated in a corner booth, cups of steaming coffee on the table before them as they waited for their sandwiches and fries. "I happened to have been shopping in the same store and saw you enter the dressing room. When the lights went out and you didn't show, well... I..." He faltered in embarrassment.

"Ran to my rescue," she interjected in a voice rife with skepticism.

Irritation flashed in his hazel eyes. "Believe what you want."

"Well, do you have reason to believe it was foul play?"

"Foul play?" He snorted. "Did you pick up that phrase from a Charlie Chan movie, Hamilton?"

"All right then, why did you suspect I was in danger?"

"I'm suspicious by nature." He picked up the cup and took several swallows of coffee.

He has nice hands, Ann reflected, observing his fingers wrapped around the cup. "Am I still in danger?"

"Agency thinks not," he answered in his irritating, succinct fashion.

The answer was too ambiguous for her satisfaction. "And what do you think, Bishop? Because if you weren't following me, someone else sure was."

"What makes you think so?"

"Because I wasn't alone in that dressing room."

She now had his full attention. "Why do you say that?"

"Someone was stalking me. I heard him."

"Hamilton, I didn't see anyone else enter that dressing room but you."

"I know what I heard. There was someone else in there."

The hazel-eyed gaze locked with hers. "How in hell did you get into this mess, Hamilton?"

The question forced her thoughts back to Clayton, and her voice softened with poignancy. "I met Clayton Burroughs four years ago. I was a fashion photographer and had gone to French Guiana on a shoot. The funny thing about it, I didn't want the assignment in the first place. I felt burned out, after five nonstop years of living out of suitcases and accumulating frequent flyer points. I didn't want to see another camera or any more gorgeous women in Gucci gowns for the rest of my life. My boss, Barney Hailey, talked me into it by promising me a month off when I finished. So I agreed."

The waitress brought their order, and as soon as she left

Bishop asked, "And how did you get mixed up with Burroughs?"

"Barney wanted authentic, outdoor shots on Devil's Island. Well, our plane developed mechanical problems, and Clayton was on the island at the time. He offered us a ride back to Kourou in his helicopter."

Deep in reverie, Ann smiled, remembering Clayton's thoughtfulness in the weeks that followed. "When we wrapped up the shoot, Barney and the crew returned to the States. Clayton coaxed me into remaining in Kourou."

"Yeah, I bet."

His suggestive tone snapped her out of her reflections. "What's that supposed to mean, Bishop? You don't get it at all. From the beginning Clayton and I were kindred souls. He was lonely. He had lost his wife and daughter fifteen years before. He thought of me as a daughter, and I envisioned him as the father I had never known."

"Until you found yourself alone with him one night with his hand up your skirt."

Her eyes flashed in anger. "You're pathetic." She started to gather up her parcels to leave.

"Okay, I apologize. Sit down and finish your lunch. So the old guy was dead from the waist down and the relationship was purely platonic. So how did a photographer get into the rocket business?"

"I doubt that you're really interested, Bishop."

"I said I was sorry." Irritation had crept into his voice. "Finish the story."

Although she doubted his sincerity, Ann did want to finish the story—for her own sake, not his. Once started on this sentimental journey, it was difficult to stop. This was the first chance she had since Clayton's death to talk about her feelings to someone…even if that someone was as cynical as Bishop. She settled back down in the seat, and after several sips of coffee Ann continued.

"Clayton was a marvelous raconteur, always relating little anecdotes about the history and culture of the country. When the time came to return to the States he persuaded me to remain as his assistant. He said intelligence and common sense were the only essentials needed to succeed in the position. Well, the whole space program was fascinating to me. I had naively believed that only the United States and the Soviets were involved with outer space. I soon discovered that European markets launched satellites as well. And after the frenetic pace of my old job, working with the relaxing atmosphere provided by Clayton soon cured me of burnout. I even began to enjoy taking photographs again."

"You gonna finish those fries?" She shook her head and handed him the plate. "What about the kid? Did Burroughs raise him?" he asked, popping a French fry into his mouth.

Her face softened in sadness. "Two years ago Clayton's son and daughter-in-law were killed in an airplane tragedy, and that's when Brandon came to live with his grandfather."

She finished her coffee and smiled. "Well, you asked for it. That's the whole story."

Whatever doubts he still harbored remained concealed behind an enigmatic gaze. "More coffee? Dessert?"

"I'm fine."

"I'll see you back to your hotel." He threw down some bills on the table, then gathered up her packages.

Once outside the mall, he flagged a cab and they returned to the Watergate.

"Mind if I come in and check your room?" he asked when they reached her door.

"I thought you said you were off the case, Bishop?"

"After the incident today, I put myself back on it, Hamilton."

He entered the room ahead of her, and after a quick check in the closet, bathroom and even under the bed, he walked to the door.

"What do you intend doing about dinner?"

"I'm intending to eat it," she said. He ignored her flippancy.

"Well, there are two selections on the menu—with me or with me watching you. Which do you prefer?"

"Are you inviting me to have dinner with you, Bishop?" she asked, amused.

"Pick you up at seven. Lock this door after me."

Her gaze followed his broad shoulders and tight buns as he walked away. "I haven't heard the click of that dead bolt, Hamilton," he called back without turning.

Smiling, she closed the door, turned the dead bolt and then slipped the chain into place.

The hotel room was lonely without Brandon. In the past two years he'd been such a big part of her life that she'd come to think of him as her son.

Ann plopped down on the bed, grabbed the telephone and dialed the number of the British Embassy, which Avery Waterman had given her. After being shifted from one extension to another, she finally heard Brandon's "hello" on the other end.

"Hi, honey, this is Ann."

"Hi, Ann." He sounded glad to hear her. And just hearing his voice lifted her spirits.

"How are you doing, sweetheart?"

"I'm having a good time, Ann. Mrs. Millen—but she said I should call her Sarah—is real nice. She's the one taking care of me. We're playing a game of Old Maid now, so I gotta go, Ann. I'll see you tomorrow."

"Yes, honey. I'll be there."

"Bye," he said, and hung up.

Ann slowly put the phone aside. She felt more depressed than ever. He sounded as if he was having such a good time that he didn't miss her. Like she never played Old Maid with him. Dear God, what if they found some legal loophole to take him away from her? It would be more than she could bear to lose Clayton and Brandon, too. They were as near to a family as she had. Ann lay back dejected, thinking what her life would be like without Brandon.

Chapter 7

Ann woke up with a start. Glancing at the clock, she saw that it was almost six o'clock. Bishop was picking her up at seven. And her instinct told her he was the kind who was always on time. She didn't have that much to choose from as to what she would wear, since she hadn't bought anything really dressy. Bishop wasn't the candlelight-and-wine type anyway, so she selected the pair of black crepe slacks and a white silk blouse with flowing sleeves cuffed at the wrists. She was glad now she'd bought the pair of black sandals, which were nothing more than a few straps on three-inch heels. They would dress up the outfit.

She took a quick shower and then brushed her hair. Fortunately the weather in French Guiana provided a year-round tan that necessitated only a light dusting of blush, powder and a touch of lip gloss. She took greater pains with her eyes. She'd photographed enough beautiful models to know that the eyes were the focal point of any woman's face. When properly made up, they could detract from a large nose, weak chin or thin lips.

As she applied the finishing touches of mascara to her eyelashes, she thought of Bishop. No doubt he preferred his females devoid of any makeup at all. She ought to paint it on heavily just to irritate him.

She dropped her arm and stared into the mirror. Why, Ann? Why do you want to irritate him? Because he's domineering, arrogant, and the…''Sexiest man I've ever known,'' she mumbled, disheartened. Face it, girl, you're scared of him. CIA! Covert missions! Megamale. Why would she want that kind of complication in her life right now? Not only was Clayton's death an emotional heartache to her, there was the problem of Brandon's guardianship to resolve. The last thing she needed was this hazel-eyed walking hunk of testosterone, whom she couldn't look at without thinking midnight kisses and the soft strains of a Sinatra love song in the background.

Doggone it, Ann. You spent too much time in that French Guianian jungle!

Promptly at seven there was a knock on the door. Ann released the chain and dead bolt and opened it. Bishop leaned on the doorframe.

''What is the sense of using a chain and dead bolt if you're going to open the door to the first person who knocks?'' he asked.

''I knew it would be you.'' He looked like a Ralph Lauren ad in a tan cashmere sport shirt and khaki slacks.

''How can you be so certain?''

''Bishop, I'd stake my life savings on a bet that you came into this world on the exact month, day, hour and minute that the doctor predicted you would.''

''I like punctuality.''

''Tell me, are you going to be your usual grumpy self, or are we going to have a pleasant conversation over dinner?''

''It all depends on what we're going to discuss.''

She grabbed a purse and shawl and stepped ahead of him. "I can hardly wait to find out."

Once outside the hotel, he hailed a cab. "You like Italian?" he asked.

"Sounds good." She glanced askance at him. Maybe dinner would be candlelight and wine after all.

He was his usual reticent self, but that was fine with Ann. She was enjoying the sights and sounds of Washington again. It seemed a lifetime since she had seen the familiar landmarks of the city.

The cab pulled up in front of a brownstone that looked no different from the other ones that lined the block. A small flight of stairs took them down to the entrance of a restaurant where a neon sign above the door glowed Sardino's.

The restaurant was delightfully heavy on atmosphere with a cozy, intimate ambiance. Red-and-white checkered tablecloths covered the tables. The smell of hot wax and spaghetti sauce permeated the air, and hazy smoke rose from empty wine bottles coated with dripping wax that served as candleholders. Breadsticks protruded from jelly glasses in the center of the tables, and there was even a strolling concertina player who nodded at Bishop when they entered. Ann loved it on sight.

Angelo Sardino greeted Bishop like a long-lost son. He gushed over Ann's beauty when Bishop introduced her, and then the owner led them to a corner booth. Very cozy. Very secluded. And very lethal in its intimacy.

"This is wonderful. I never found a really good Italian restaurant in Kourou. Seems like everything was French cooking. I hope the food lives up to the atmosphere."

"I'm strictly a spaghetti man," Bishop said, "so I can't vouch for anything else. But I've never heard any complaints."

"Do you live in D.C., Bishop?"

"It's Mike, Ann."

She laughed lightly. "So you do have a first name."

"We don't throw our names around on a mission. Never know who might overhear."

"You mean you work undercover, too?"

"No. Our mission is usually to get in and out in a hurry."

At that moment a waitress came over to take their order. "Glad to see you back home safely, Mike."

"Thanks, Nina. How are you doing?"

"Getting married in two months. Hope you and the squad are in town for it."

"If we are, we'll be there. How's Mama doing?"

The girl's eyes saddened. "Missing Tony. We all are. Poppa covers it up better than the rest of us do. My wedding plans are helping Mama to get through it."

"That's good. Danny's a lucky guy. Nina, this is Ann Hamilton. Nina's Angelo's daughter," he explained to Ann.

Ann smiled warmly. "Hi, Nina." For a moment Ann had been afraid she would have to go through the awkwardness of meeting an ex-girlfriend. Not that there was anything other than business between her and Bishop. It just would have been uncomfortable.

"Glad to meet you, Ann. Hope you know you're out with the best guy in the world."

"Other than Danny, of course," Ann teased.

Nina's eyes widened with pleasure. "Do you know Danny?"

"No, but it kind of shows when you mention his name."

Nina giggled. "Am I that obvious? Are you ready to order?"

"The spaghetti comes recommended, so I'll try that."

"Sausage or meatballs?" **Nina asked.**

Ann arched a brow and looked at Bishop for his pref-
erence.

"Meatballs," he said. "House dressing on the salad,
and a bottle of Chianti."

That was Bishop all right. Precise. Succinct. Why waste
words even among friends?

"They all seem to know you very well," Ann said as
soon as the girl left. "You must come here often."

His mouth slashed into a grim line. "Yeah. Ann's
brother was a member of our squad. He was killed last
month in Beirut."

"Oh, I'm so sorry. So obviously D.C.'s your home."

"I keep a small, walk-up apartment. Nothing fancy. A
place to sleep when I'm in town. You planning on returning permanently to the States?"

"I think so. As soon as I settle this custody battle over
Brandon, I'll go back to Kourou and pack up."

Mike shrugged. "I wouldn't worry about Brandon's
custody. Sounds like a slam dunk to me."

Her hopes soared. "You really think so? Mr. Waterman
didn't sound too encouraging."

"He's a priss. Are you planning on legally adopting the
kid?"

"If I'm allowed to. I don't know the rules in a situation
like this, but I'm going to get a lawyer and find out. If I
can't, I'll have to settle for just being his guardian, but I
would love to legally have him as a son."

"No boyfriend to object."

"That's right. Even if I had one, it wouldn't do him any
good to try. I love Brandon. What about you, Bish…ah,
Mike? First night back in town. I'd have thought you'd
want to hook up with a girlfriend instead of baby-sitting
me. After all, this dinner tonight is in the line of duty."

"If it were, I wouldn't have brought you here. These
are friends. I don't mix business and pleasure."

The irritation in his tone was a slap on the hand. At the same time it pleased her to find out he was attracted enough to her that he'd ask her out to dinner.

"I'm surprised you'd want to go dinner with me. I recall you telling me what a big pain in the rear end I am."

He chuckled. "I'm masochistic by nature."

"You're so flattering, Bishop." Couldn't he ever say something pleasant or complimentary? She snatched a bread stick and took a bite from it.

Nina came back with a plate of antipasto and a bottle of wine, winked at Ann, then left hurriedly.

"Is that a smirk or a grin you're wearing, Bishop?"

"It's a grin," he said, and filled their glasses.

"What's so amusing?"

"Your body language. You're pissed."

"I am not. It's simply that you can be so irritating at times."

"I wouldn't have asked you to dinner if I didn't want to be with you."

"Then, why couldn't you have said that?"

"I thought you were smart enough to have figured that out for yourself."

"Why should I have thought any differently? You indicated you were protecting me. The dinner invitation came under that mantle of responsibility."

"So I stretched the truth. I'm on my own time."

"Stretched? It was an out-and-out lie."

"You saying you wouldn't have come otherwise?"

"I didn't say that." Frustrated, she took another bite of the bread stick. Fearing she might resemble Bugs Bunny chomping on a carrot, she quickly put the stick on the bread plate. "What?" she asked, when he stared bemused at her.

"Some guy do you wrong, Ann?"

"Why do you think that?"

"I'm trying to figure why a woman with your looks feels so insecure around a man."

"Insecure? That's ridiculous." He was really pushing her buttons now. She grabbed a pepper from the antipasto.

"Hold up, don't—"

His warning came too late. She had already taken a hefty bite of it. Suddenly her throat felt on fire, her eyes began to water and her mouth gaped open as she tried to suck in air. Groping for her glass, she literally gulped down the wine.

"I tried to warn you."

"What was it?" she gasped, when she was finally able to speak.

"Mama Sardino's personal hot pepper recipe." He refilled her wineglass. "You okay?"

"Yes." Then she began to laugh. "I must have looked ridiculous. You must think I *am* a real pain in the rear end, Mike."

He picked up his glass of wine and tipped it toward her in a gesture of a toast. "You'd be surprised what I think of you, Ann Hamilton."

Her eyes swept his face, trying to read what lay behind that ambiguous comment. "At one time I'd have said I don't much care, but now…" She picked up her glass and took a sip of the wine. "I have to admit I'm curious."

"Okay. Great eyes, long legs, which I've yet to see because you've always been in pants, nice boobs and a trim little tush."

"Bishop, I wasn't referring to physical characteristics." She reached for the bread stick again.

"I was getting to that. Smart, witty and insecure around men. I even detect a dislike in general for the gender. You wouldn't be… I mean you're not—"

"No, I am not gay, if that's what you're implying. Why would you even think that?"

"Father died while you were still young. You're twenty-eight. You've never married. Never had a steady or live-in boyfriend. You chose a profession that centered on beautiful women. Your closest relationship with the opposite sex is a six-year-old boy and a man who was old enough to be your father. And right now you're sitting there all uptight as if you expect that I'm about to jump your bones any minute."

She'd heard enough and reached for her purse to leave. "Don't even think it, Ann. You're going to remain and enjoy your dinner. You asked what I was thinking. I told you."

"I might have known your candidness would be rude and insulting." Fretful that if she got up to leave, he'd manhandle her the way he did on the airplane, she remained seated.

"Well, you're wrong, Bishop. I do not hate the male population. And just because I don't hop into bed with every guy that hits on me doesn't make me a lesbian. Furthermore, I've had a couple relationships with men. They just didn't work out.

"I figure when the right man comes along, I'll know it. Until then I have no desire to accommodate men like you, whose only interest is getting into my pants so they can hang another scalp on their coup stick. And if I appear uptight with you, Bishop, it's because you intimidate. That's your forte. Who and what you are. Mr. Macho. Mr. CIA. Me Tarzan, you Jane. How old are you, Bishop?"

"Thirty."

"Well as for your accusations about my sex life, I'd stake every penny I have that at thirty you've *never* had a serious relationship with a female in your life. Oh, sure, you've had plenty of one-night stands. No doubt there are enough sapless females in the world who'd line up for that privilege. But their names are left blank in your diary,

Bishop, because you don't remember them—much less how to spell them—the morning after.''

Throughout her tirade his expression never altered. Finally he picked up the wine bottle and with a smile—that made her grind her teeth to keep from snarling—he leaned forward.

''More wine?''

''Why not!'' she exclaimed with reckless abandon, and reached for her glass.

Fortunately, Nina brought their salads, which gave Ann something to do other than rant at Mike. She forked a piece of lettuce and popped it into her mouth. It was delicious. As was the spaghetti that followed.

They topped off the meal with a tangy Italian trifle with a lemon custard filling. Ann ordered a cup of cappuccino while Mike opted for black coffee laced with brandy.

Ann had no desire to end the delicious dinner with another argument with Mike, so she directed the conversation to a more casual topic and found out he and the squad were on leave for the next thirty days.

''So what are you planning on doing with your free time?''

''I have a cabin in northern Wisconsin,'' he said. ''I thought I'd go up and do some fishing.''

''No family, Mike?''

''Nope. Folks died three years ago. No siblings. Got a couple cousins I get together with on occasion. What about you?''

''No family—not even cousins.'' She grinned at him. ''Of course, you probably know that already. My ex-boss, Barney Hailey, is the closest thing I have to a Dutch uncle. Sounds like we're a couple of 'poor little lambs who have lost our way.' ''

He raised his glass. '' 'Baa, baa, baa.' ''

They clinked their glasses together and broke into laughter. "What about the rest of the squad, Mike?"

"The guys with folks here in the States have gone home. Williams and Bledsoe went back to England."

"Who's married on the squad?"

"None of us."

That was a shocker to her. "Out of six, none of you are married. That's unusual."

"With our jobs, we aren't exactly good husband material."

They did live dangerously. She regretted the nasty way she talked to him. He could very well be killed on the next mission he went on.

"You mentioned Nina's brother was killed. What kind of an accident was it?"

"One on his part, apparently. He must have left his guard down. His throat was slit."

"Oh, dear God! On a mission?"

"Not actually *on* the mission. He was murdered later."

"Murdered!" Maybe it was too much wine, but Ann's head began to spin. Clayton murdered. Tony Sardino murdered. How did her life suddenly get so enmeshed with murders? CIA. Kidnappings. Stalkings.

And the equally dangerous Mike Bishop. His sensuality was lethal. No matter how attracted she was to him, he was right in the middle of it. Living on the edge was his kind of life, and she wanted no part of it. Once Clayton's funeral was over and she had custody of Brandon, she'd get as far away from these people and Washington, D.C., as she could.

However, thinking about it all did stir up the events of that afternoon in her mind. Maybe she had imagined there was someone else in that dressing room. In her frame of mind over Clayton's death, the incident with those abductors, and then having to relinquish Brandon, it very likely could have been her imagination screwing up her head. Mike seemed convinced there'd been no one but her in the room, and he was a trained agent.

They rode back to the hotel in silence and he insisted on seeing her to the door of her room. It was very awkward to try and thank him for a dinner, which, despite her haranguing him, had been enjoyable, and she knew would remain memorable to her.

He unlocked the door and then dropped the key into her hand. "I suppose it would be foolish of me to suggest I come in."

"I wish you wouldn't, Mike. The temptation would be too great to resist."

"Yeah, you're right. You're not the kind of woman who goes for a one-night stand."

"Or is crazy enough to let herself get involved with a guy who lives on the edge like you do."

"Yeah, right again. There's no room in my life for anything other than a casual relationship."

She reached out a hand. His hand closed around hers with a warmth as stimulating as it was pleasing. "So, I guess this is where I tell you thanks for everything. Kourou. Dinner. Putting up with me when I'm at my worst."

He didn't release her hand. "You don't have to make excuses, Ann. You've got a lot of grit. I know the problem with the kid will work out, too."

"Take care of yourself, Mike, and the other guys on the squad. I'm grateful to all of you."

She tried to turn away to enter, but he held fast to her hand. "Dammit, there's only one way to say goodbye to you, Ann."

Pulling her into his arms, he swallowed her gasp of surprise as his lips covered hers. For an instant she thought of resisting, and then, caught up in the emotional depth of her true feelings, she settled into the kiss, and their mouths found a fit.

His lips were firm and warm, the kiss hot and arousing. Her whole being flooded with a stimulating urgency of pure lust. An urgency that settled in her groin and thighs and caused her to shift restlessly in search of appeasement.

Caught up in her own emotional, as well as physical, need, she slipped her arms around his neck, clinging to the rock-solid hardness of his body as she matched his intensity with her own. The thought of the latent strength of that body became an added turn-on. She'd been kissed before—or had she? Certainly no man's kisses had ever tapped an instant need for sex as this kiss did. If he didn't break it off—because she wasn't going to be the one to do so—they would surely end up on the bed despite the futility of any hope for a relationship between them. Who in hell cared? She couldn't think beyond this moment— she didn't want to.

She felt bereft when he broke the kiss. Reaching up, he gripped her wrists and lowered her arms from around his neck. Then he stepped away, and Ann raised her eyelids. She labored to draw a breath, and gazed up at him, her eyes drugged with passion.

"You make a man forget his good intentions, lady. This will probably be the dumbest thing I've ever done. Goodbye, Ann."

"Goodbye, Mike."

Her heart was thudding in her chest, her legs shaking as she closed the door. With trembling fingers she turned the dead bolt and slipped the chain into place. This time to keep herself from running after him.

Chapter 8

Ann spent a restless night thinking about Mike. The next morning as she dressed for a jog he was still on her mind.

There are many interesting people who come and go in one's life, and Mike Bishop was merely one of the passing parade. Admittedly, she felt a strong physical attraction toward him—his kiss curled her toes.

But there was a lot more to life than sex. In a weak moment she had almost abandoned the principles she'd lived by since she learned the big difference between a man and a woman.

And his kiss last night sure proved there was a big difference between Mike Bishop and other men she had known.

Thank goodness he had the common sense to step out of her life before they became more deeply involved with each other. As it was, it would still take time to get over him.

Mike Bishop was not the kind you could wipe out of your mind with a single stroke of a brush.

She left the hotel and headed for the Washington Monument. She'd have time to jog there and back before her meeting with Waterman. If all things went well, she should be reunited with Brandon today.

You see, Ann, things aren't all doom-and-gloom.

D.C. wasn't quite awake yet. Even so, there were a few joggers like her getting in a morning run before the oppressive heat and traffic closed in. By the time she reached the Washington Monument and made her turn to head back to the hotel, she was feeling the effects of the run. She hadn't exercised for the past several days and was paying for it now. Tempted to rest, she moved over toward the grass and slowed down to almost a walk.

Another jogger appeared behind her, and when he started to pass, he suddenly grabbed her. "Don't scream, lady, or I'll shove this knife into you." He started to force her toward the elm trees lining the walk.

Her adrenaline kicked in. In the last couple days she'd had too much of being menaced by brutes. She screamed and began to struggle with him. He was stronger than she and was winning the contest when Ann succeeded in poking him in the eye with her finger.

He cursed and dropped the knife as he covered his eye. It was enough to enable her to twist out of his grasp and start to run. The attacker grabbed for her again, and succeeded in tripping her. Ann twisted her ankle and, screaming for help, she fell to the ground.

"Hey, what's going on?" a voice yelled from nearby.

"Bitch!" he snarled. The attacker picked up the knife and took off as a young couple ran over to her.

"Are you okay?" the man asked. His companion was already on a cell phone.

"I think so," Ann said. "I'm sure glad you two showed up."

"Let me help you," the man said when Ann hobbled over to lean against a tree.

Once she was seated, the woman handed Ann the bottle of water she'd been carrying. "Here, I think you need this more than I do."

A squad car showed up in answer to the 911 call, and one of the officers took the statements and names and address of the young couple. Ann thanked them for their help, and they left when a medical unit arrived. The ankle injury appeared minor, but the paramedics advised her to have it X-rayed for her own peace of mind.

Ann couldn't offer too much of a description of the attacker other than he was a few inches taller than her, dressed in black, had a thin face, dark hair and a deep voice. It had happened too fast to remember much more than that.

"There've been several sexual attacks on female joggers in the past couple months, Miss Hamilton," one of the officers said after taking her statement. "We've been issuing warnings for women not to jog alone."

"I'm a visitor to your city, Officer. I wasn't aware of the warning, but if I told you what I've gone through in the past few days, you wouldn't believe me."

"Just the same, you're lucky that couple appeared when they did or the outcome might have ended more drastically than a sore ankle. He not only rapes his victims, but cuts them up pretty badly to disfigure them. You're one of the few victims who have survived virtually unscathed. Do you want a ride to the hospital?"

"No. My ankle feels better already."

"Then would you be willing to come to police headquarters and describe the attacker to an artist?"

"Well, I'll do my best. As I said, it all happened pretty fast so I didn't really get a long look at him."

Ann spent about thirty minutes with the talented artist

who was able to reproduce a facsimile from her vague descriptions. Surprisingly, when they were through, the sketch did bear a remarkable resemblance to the attacker. The only thing she really couldn't recall with any distinction were his eyes. The artist drew several different shapes, but Ann couldn't offer any more help.

Before leaving, they had her go through several large albums of known rapists, but none matched the description of the attacker.

By the time she was through, the patrol officers offered to drive her back to her hotel. Her ankle had begun aching slightly, and it was nearing the time for an appointment she had at the CIA.

"I'd appreciate that," she said.

Returning to her room, Ann showered and was ready when the CIA limo arrived to take her to the CIA headquarters in Langley, Virginia.

The complex was entirely different from the building she'd been brought to in the previous meetings with Baker and Waterman. The grounds were landscaped with maples, lovely flower beds and ground cover.

If it weren't for the tight security to get in—which involved being photographed and pinned with a visitor pass to say the least—the headquarters and surrounding grounds could have passed for the campus of a small college.

For some inexplicable reason she felt a lump in her throat as she looked at the huge granite seal inlaid on the floor of the main headquarters, the symbolic emblem of the Central Intelligence Agency.

Because the Agency had always been so repugned on television and the movies, she had never given much thought to the men and women who risked their lives to protect this country. Now she had faces and names to give

them some identity. And once again the image of Mike
Bishop loomed in her memory.

While Ann waited for someone to escort her upstairs,
she glanced over at the north wall of the lobby where an
inscription read "IN HONOR OF THOSE MEMBERS OF
THE CENTRAL INTELLIGENCE AGENCY WHO GAVE
THEIR LIVES IN THE SERVICE OF THEIR COUN-
TRY."

Framed by an American flag on the left and the CIA
flag on the right were rows of stars representing the agents
who made the ultimate sacrifice for their country. At least
one of them now had a face and name to her—the image
of a young man of Italian descent named Tony Sardino.

Upon seeing the approach of Jeff Baker, she rose hurriedly to her feet, and winced from the shock of pain.

"Miss Hamilton, a pleasure to see you," Baker said.
His ruddy face grimaced in a frown. "What's wrong? Are
you ill?"

"It's nothing serious. I hurt my ankle this morning."

"Would you like a wheelchair?"

"Heavens, no! I just jumped up too fast."

As he took her arm and led her to the elevator, Ann told
him about her incident in the park.

Avery Waterman was waiting for them in his office. As
soon as she entered, he rose to his feet. As usual he was
tastefully garbed without a wrinkle in sight or a gray hair
out of place.

"A pleasure to see you again, Miss Hamilton. Please
have a chair."

Ann sat down, and Baker took the chair next to her.

"We've received word from the British Embassy that
the body of Clayton Burroughs has been returned to England and will be interred tomorrow in the family vault."

"Tomorrow! Then I must hurry and make my arrangements. I intend to be there."

"We assumed as much and have taken the liberty of making arrangements for you to accompany Brandon Burroughs, Miss Hamilton."

"Oh, thank you, Mr. Waterman. I really appreciate that. I'm sure there was some red tape to cut through. Has there been any further word on when he will be released into my custody?"

"Not at this time. The British State Department is pursuing it and said you can remain with Brandon until you return to the States. The lad will have to remain in England until his custody is resolved."

Ann shot to her feet. "You mean there's a possibility that he won't be coming back to the United States with me? They can't do that. Clayton's will clearly states that his wishes are for me to have custody of Brandon."

"Then it should be resolved with the reading of the will. You must try to understand their position, Miss Hamilton. Clayton Burroughs was a wealthy man. If Brandon Burroughs is his primary beneficiary, the boy stands to inherit a great deal of money. You can't blame the British government for making certain no one else will profit from that inheritance."

Ann felt on the verge of hysteria. "Surely you don't think my interest in Brandon is because of his inheritance?"

"I don't, Miss Hamilton. And frankly I doubt the British government thinks so either. They are merely being cautious. It's a minor delay, and we'll do everything in our power to expedite the situation."

"Thank you."

Waterman's phone buzzed and he picked it up. "Yes, send him in, please."

The door opened and Brandon stepped into the room. At the sight of him, Ann's heart swelled with love.

His face lit with joy. "Ann," he cried, and ran to her.

She sank to her knees with outstretched arms, and the youngster ran into them. For a long moment they hugged and kissed.

"I've missed you, sweetheart."

"I've missed you, too," he said. "When can I come and live with you, Ann? Sarah is very nice, but I want to be with you."

His words were music to her ears. The last few days had been so full of fears and insecurities that she had even begun to doubt his love. But now he was here in her arms and nothing else mattered.

"Miss Hamilton, your flight leaves at eight o'clock tonight. If there is anything you'll need for the trip, I suggest you get it now, or if you prepare a list, I can have one of the staff get it for you. We will handle your checkout at the hotel, or do you prefer to keep the room until you return?"

"No, I prefer to be checked out. If there's a problem about Brandon's custody, our return could be delayed for days. Thank you again for all your trouble. Are we free to leave here now, Mr. Waterman?"

"Of course. We'll have a limo at your hotel at six o'clock. I hope that is sufficient time for you to get ready."

Ann stood up and took Brandon's hand. "I guess we better get going, sweetheart, if we intend to be on time. Thank you, Mr. Waterman, for all your help." She remembered Baker's presence. The American official had not said a word since they entered the room. She nodded to him. "And you, too, Mr. Baker."

"Have a pleasant flight, Miss Hamilton. I wish it was under different circumstances."

"We both do, Mr. Baker," she said.

As soon as they left, Baker and Waterman exchanged meaningful glances. "I don't like this," Baker said. He left the room.

Jeff Baker returned to his office, picked up the telephone and punched in numbers. When his call was answered, he said, "I have to talk to you right away. Get over to Langley on the double."

Chapter 9

Mike sat down and waited while Baker finished a conversation on the phone. When he hung up, Baker got to his feet and walked around the desk.

"Mike, I'm sending you out."

He and the squad needed a rest, and they were going to get one. "The team's on leave, remember? They're all over the place by now. You caught me practically going out the door. I'm heading back to Wisconsin for a couple weeks. I intend to just lie around and get in some fishing."

"Forget the team. I'm just sending you."

"Like hell you are! Beirut, Afghanistan, Iraq. I'm burned out. You've got other agents."

"You're familiar with this one. It's the Burroughs case."

Mike had spent a restless night thinking about Ann Hamilton—and that kiss. The thought of it began licking at his groin again. "The team completed our mission and we're out of it."

''Not anymore. The whole damn thing reeks of three-day-old fish. The Hamilton woman was attacked this morning while she was out jogging.''

If Baker wanted his attention, he just got it. Thank God for his training. Despite the fact that his stomach had just taken a giant leap to his throat, Mike asked casually, ''Attacked?'' So maybe his voice sounded like he hadn't reached puberty. He sucked in a deep breath and shoved the lump back down into the churning tank of stomach acid that was burning his guts. Objectivity, Bishop. Don't lose your objectivity.

''What happened?''

''Seems Miss Hamilton was jogging this morning at the Ellipsis. Some guy came along and threatened her with a knife. She fought him off, and when a couple of joggers came along the guy took off.''

His heart had begun thumping painfully in his chest. ''Was she hurt?''

''It shook her up a little, but she got off with just a twisted ankle.''

''You think the attack had something to do with Burroughs's death?''

''Could be just coincidence. The D.C. police said there have been other attacks near there. The son of a bitch rapes and disfigures his victims.''

''But you aren't buying that theory.''

''Waterman is, but I didn't stay alive in this business by believing in coincidence, Mike. I go with my gut feelings. I figure the lady knows something.''

''You think she's lying to us?''

''Not necessarily. It could be something she doesn't even know she knows. It might be bits of information she can't connect. But the killer might figure she could put the pieces together and finger him.''

''So what do you have in mind?''

"Hamilton and the boy are booked on an eight-o'clock London flight out of here tonight to attend Burroughs's funeral. The limo will pick them up at six. I want you with them. What will you be packing?"

"I suppose a suit since there'll be a funeral, shaving gear, a couple pair of socks and shorts—an Uzi pistol and a Trident."

"Trident? Why the knife?"

"Didn't you tell me Hamilton's attacker had a knife? If the bastard's an up-close-and-personal kind of guy, I'll be glad to oblige him."

"You really are a killing machine, aren't you, Bishop?"

"You trained me, sir. Just make sure no air marshal gets any ideas to search me."

"I'll get you cleared through the security, then you're on your own. You've been trained to blend into the background. So blend."

Baker got up and walked him to the door. "Good luck, Mike," he said as they shook hands. "Let's hope that maybe this morning's attack was just coincidence. I don't want to hear that anything happened to that woman or that boy."

"You've got that right, sir."

Mike left headquarters and went back to his apartment. He took a shower and dressed. It didn't take long to pack the few belongings he intended to take along. He even remembered a shirt and tie.

Next he loaded his pistol and got the Trident from his gear. Rolling up the right pant leg of the khakis he was wearing, he put on a leg holster for the pistol, and then rolled up the other pant leg and put on a sheath for the knife.

Mike stepped back and checked himself out in the mirror. Maybe the three of them would look like a family on vacation to the other passengers.

Yeah, right! A person would have to be freaking blind not to figure him as a Fed or a cop, but at least neither weapon bulged.

After throwing a shoulder holster into his bag to wear at the funeral, a couple of extra clips for the gun, he locked up the bag that was small enough to carry on the airplane. Then, grabbing a lightweight jacket he left. It was exactly five o'clock when he tapped on Ann's door at the Watergate.

Her surprise was evident. ''Mike, what a surprise to see you. I wasn't expecting you.''

''The Agency didn't call?''

''Why no. What about?''

''May I come in?'' She nodded and moved aside.

Mike stepped in and closed the door. Brandon was stretched out on the bed, lying on his stomach with his chin propped up in his hands. At the sight of Mike, he jumped off the bed. ''Mike! Is Rick and Pete with you?''

''No, they went back to England.''

''We're going to England, too. Aren't we, Ann?''

''Yes, we are,'' Ann said. ''Something tells me Mr. Bishop is aware of that. Aren't you, Mike?''

''Yes, that's why I'm here. How's your ankle? Heard you had an accident.''

''It's fine. Nothing serious.''

''The ankle or the accident? Can I talk to you privately, Ann?''

She looked around the room. ''I guess it will have to be in the bathroom. Sweetheart,'' she said to Brandon, ''go back and watch your television show. Mike and I have some business to discuss.''

Once in the bathroom, Mike closed the door. ''I'll be going to England with you.''

''You mean as a watchdog.''

''Call it what you wish.''

"I don't need a watchdog, Mike. I'm sure I'll be perfectly safe in England."

"Ann, use your common sense. Clayton Burroughs was murdered in Kourou. And even though he's dead, whoever was responsible came after you and the kid. Why?"

"Maybe they didn't know Clayton was dead. He was a wealthy man and they may have just planned on holding us for ransom."

"Yeah, right," he said. "What about yesterday morning in the mall? You were terrorized there."

"You said it was my imagination. Are you saying you lied to me?"

"Yesterday I did think it was your imagination. I didn't see anyone go into that dressing room after you entered. I figured if it wasn't your imagination maybe a woman had been in there when you entered, and could have been just as scared as you were."

He didn't believe that explanation any more than she did. "Besides, in thinking it over, I lost sight of the dressing room for ten seconds when I had to step around a floor display. Someone could have sneaked in then."

"Oh, now you tell me. Yesterday you were adamant that no one entered that room after I did."

"I'm trying to be objective, Ann. Now, considering the incident this morning, I'm convinced someone wants you out of the way."

"The police said that man has attacked other women."

"Did you ever hear of copycats? It's a good way to knock off someone when there's a serial killer or rapist operating in the vicinity."

He could see his words had begun to sink in. Those gorgeous violet eyes of hers were widening with every word he spoke. "Why would anyone think I know anything? If I did, I would have revealed it at once. I told the CIA everything I know."

''We think that you may know something significant and don't realize it. It's all theory, but the Agency thinks you're at risk.'' He hesitated, and then added, ''I think you're at risk, Ann. I let you push me away the other night because emotionally that was the easiest way out. No strain. No pain. I won't let that happen again. You've touched something in me, and I'm involved whether I want to be or not. But the only way I can protect you is not to let my emotions mess things up again.''

''Mike, what almost happened between us last night makes it very awkward to be with you. If your agency wants to protect me, I prefer they use a different agent.'' She tried to soften the words with a weak smile. ''I can't say it's not personal, because it's very personal. I think you understand.''

''I think you don't. Anything that's gone between us in the past remains there. I'm a professional on an assigned mission. That means I don't muddy up the water with personal feelings.

''In case you weren't aware in that little French Guiana Shangri-la you existed in, lady, it's a dangerous world out there. Our agents have their hands full. The Agency's sending me because I'm familiar with the background of this situation. So right now I'm the only thing that could be standing between you having your head blown off or your throat slit. You're just going to have to grin and bear it. If you don't cooperate, you could be endangering Brandon's life, as well. So I go, or you don't go. It's that simple. End of discussion, Miss Hamilton.''

''As usual, Bishop, your ultimatum leaves me little choice.''

''I assume you're packed and ready to leave. The limo's due shortly.''

Those violet eyes were flashing danger signals, but he had to give her credit for not smashing him in the mouth.

"You know, Bishop, you were easier to tolerate when you kept your mouth shut."

She opened the door, and he started to follow her. She slammed it back in his face as she stormed out.

"Dammit!" She'd done that on purpose. He grabbed his nose and checked it in the mirror. At least it wasn't bleeding. Maybe she didn't need anyone to protect her after all.

Ann was helping Brandon on with his shoes when Mike came out of the bathroom. She started to close up a tiny child's suitcase with large paste-on letters that spelled B R A N D O N across the top of it.

"Couldn't you have packed the kid's clothes in one of these other suitcases?"

"These aren't clothes. They're coloring books, crayons, story books and treats to snack on."

"Don't you think the kid should try and sleep instead during the night?"

"Tomorrow's another day, Bishop."

"So it is, Miss Scarlet. So it is." He shoved his own bag under his arm and picked up two more of hers.

"How in hell did you manage to buy out Washington in just a couple of days?"

"I'm well organized," she said, tucking Brandon's case under his other arm.

When they left the room, he could only hope they didn't run into any terrorists in the elevator.

Chapter 10

Mike was seated directly across the aisle from Ann and Brandon. They were in first class, so there were fewer people he had to concentrate on. Not that he figured anything would happen on the plane. And, since it was an overnight flight, everyone slept most of the way to London.

As soon as they landed, he took them straight to the British State Department. The funeral service and interrment, scheduled for three o'clock that afternoon, would be held at the site of the Burroughs's vault. He hated letting Ann out of his sight until then, but she would be as safe there as she would in a hotel room with him. Probably a damn sight safer considering how his testosterone level soared whenever he thought about her.

He checked into the hotel Baker had reserved for him and left a wake-up call for one o'clock. It took him fifteen minutes to shower and shave, then he hit the sack. A few hours later the buzzing telephone woke him up at one o'clock.

The limo was waiting when he arrived to accompany them. Ann came out of the building holding Brandon's hand. She was dressed in a plain sleeveless black dress with a round neckline. The hem came to the top of her knees, a single strand of pearls was around her neck, tiny pearls at her ears, and her blond hair was swept up and pinned at the top of her head. Classy and simple. Princess Grace Kelly. Audrey Hepburn. Not like any of the trashy-looking actresses of today who figured they had to have their boobs hanging out or their bare butts showing to look sexy. She didn't need any of those kind of gimmicks. One look at her and his fingers began itching to get at those pins in her hair and the zipper at the back of the dress.

And her legs had been worth the wait. Most men were "T and A" guys. Not him. Nothing turned him on like a good pair of legs. And Ann had a good pair of legs. Long and tan running clear down to the painted toenails peeking out from under a couple of black straps that passed as shoes.

He lifted his gaze and saw she was staring at him with a surprised look. "What?" he asked.

"You look very handsome in a suit and tie, Bishop."

"And you look even better in a dress than you do in slacks, Hamilton."

"How do I look, Mike?" Brandon asked.

Mike had forgotten about the kid. He was dressed in a black suit with long pants. "I'd say you look pretty spiffy in that suit, dude."

Brandon looked at Ann. "What does spiffy mean?"

"It means you look good."

Brandon grinned. "Ann bought it for me today," he said, climbing into the limo.

"Today?" Mike grabbed Ann's arm as she was about to step into the car. "You went shopping today?"

"It was just a quick trip, Mike. I decided short pants weren't proper for a funeral."

"Who in hell pays any attention to what a kid is wearing? I told you not to go anywhere without me. Dammit, Ann, why didn't you call me?"

"It's over and done with. Nothing happened."

"This time."

She stepped in and sat down. He slammed the door and then climbed into the front seat next to the driver.

"I wouldn't be here if the Agency didn't believe it was necessary. Either you start cooperating, or I'm putting that trim little tush of yours back on a plane to the States right now."

"Don't issue orders to me, Bishop. And watch your language in front of Brandon. Can't you see you're upsetting him?"

"He'll be a lot more upset if you get hurt. From now on you don't take a pee without me, understand?"

She glared at him, turned her head, and proceeded to look out the window.

He took it as a yes.

The route wound along the spectacular beauty of the rugged coastline. Foamy waves lapped at the rocky boulders swarming with hundreds of seagulls lazing in the bright sunshine.

After a forty-five-minute drive they arrived at the cemetery where several rows of chairs had been set up under a canopy in front of a granite mausoleum bearing the Burroughs name.

Mike appraised the crowd at once and came up with a head count of forty-two. He stood back and tried to appear inconspicuous as the assembled mourners greeted Ann and Brandon.

Suddenly he stiffened to attention when one of the men rushed up to Ann and threw his arms around her. The kiss he gave her looked anything but casual. What the hell was the guy doing? This was a funeral for cripes' sake. He sure wasn't acting like he was in mourning.

Who in hell was he? The man looked Latin—Argentinean or Brazilian. Probably late forties or mid-fifties. Smooth. Handsome. Custom-made suits. Big bucks. Poloponies rich.

Mike shifted his gaze to the parked cars, looking for a Lamborghini or at least a Porsche. A red Ferrari convertible stood out among the row of black or gray limos like a peacock in a flock of pigeons. No surprise there.

He didn't like the way the guy was cozying up to Ann, and started to move toward them. An announcement was made requesting everyone to be seated. The Latin lover took Ann's arm and sat down next to her, so Mike backed up and took a seat in the last row where he had an open-angled view of her.

The minister began eulogizing Clayton Burroughs, but Mike focused his attention on Ann in the front row. He could tell the clergyman's words were hitting her hard. Her head was bowed and Gilbert Roland—or whatever the hell the guy's name was—slipped his arm around her shoulders.

He felt like a bastard. He'd forgotten the personal grief she was suffering. When he'd picked her up he'd been distracted by how good she looked. Then he'd come down on her about going shopping. His attitude was only adding to her misery.

He wasn't the right man to pull this kind of duty. He'd never been a people person—a touchy-feely kind of guy. Tony would have been great at this. Tony was great with people. That's why everybody loved him. Yeah, everybody but the bastard who slit his throat!

Don't go there, Bishop. This isn't the time or place.

As soon as the service was over he got up and approached Ann. "Are you ready to leave, Miss Hamilton?"

"Yes. Mike. Will you take Brandon to the car while I say goodbye to Mr. DeVilles?"

"Ann, I haven't seen you in weeks," DeVilles said. "We have so much to talk over. I insist you let me drive you." He turned to Mike. "Take the child back and inform them Miss Hamilton will return after dinner."

"Ricardo, you don't understand. Mike isn't my chauffeur. He's…ah a—"

"Family friend, DeVilles. Sorry, but Ann's having dinner with me. Tough luck, pal." He took her by the arm and Brandon by the hand and led them away.

As soon as they reached the car, she put Brandon inside. "I have to talk to Mike a minute, sweetheart. I'll be right back."

She stepped away from the car and turned on him. "What is the meaning of this, Bishop? There was no excuse for your rudeness." She was so angry she looked ready to strike him.

"Who is that DeVilles? He looks like a pimp."

"Ricardo DeVilles was a close friend and business acquaintance of Clayton's. And he's a friend of mine. Who do you think you are to insult my friends like this?"

"Like he didn't insult me."

"Based on the way you approached me and asked me if I was ready to leave, Ricardo made a logical mistake in thinking that you were probably my driver. His rudeness was unintentional. While yours, Bishop, was deliberate."

"Well, the guy was all over you. My job is to protect you. So I'll apologize the next time I see him."

"There won't be a next time. I never should have agreed to this arrangement. I want you out of my life, Bishop. I made the mistake of listening to you, but neither you nor the CIA have any right to interfere in my life. I can take care of myself. Furthermore, I have decided to go to dinner with Ricardo.''

She stormed away from him, walked over and talked to DeVilles who had just climbed into the seat of a red Ferrari.

Mike opened the front door of the limo and watched her as she spoke to DeVilles for a few minutes and then headed back to them. He sat down and closed the door.

The limo driver jumped out quickly and opened the rear door for her. Once she was seated, he closed the door then returned to the driver's seat. He gave Mike a disgusted look, then turned the ignition key.

So the guy thought he was a bastard. Welcome to the club, pal.

"Sweetheart, I'm going out to dinner with Mr. DeVilles tonight," she said to Brandon.

"Can I come?"

"Not tonight, dear. But I won't leave until after you've eaten.''

"Why do you have to have dinner with him, anyway? I don't like him. Why don't you and me and Mike have dinner?''

A three-point basket for the kid! Mike fought hard to contain a grin.

"Brandon! Shame on you. Mr. DeVilles has always been nice to you. Why don't you like him?''

"'Cause I don't. He's got sneaky eyes. I don't like people with sneaky eyes.''

A slam dunk. The L.A. Lakers ought to recruit this kid.

"Hamilton, they always say when it comes to people one should trust the instincts of kids and dogs," Mike said.

"It's a little late for any pearls of wisdom from you, Bishop.''

She turned her attention to enjoying the view, and they rode in silence for the next few minutes.

Suddenly the driver mumbled, "What's this bloke doing?"

Mike glanced across him to see a large gray van attempting to pass them on the narrow road. The car almost pushed them off the road. There was a loud popping sound when one of their tires blew out and the rear of the limo began to fishtail out of control.

Ann screamed and threw her arms protectively around Brandon. The grind of gravel under the wheels was a piercing screech to their ears when the car spun and swung back onto the shoulder of the road. For the span of a held breath, the spinning rear wheels of the car hung suspended over the side. The rocking vehicle threatened to topple to the rocks below until the thrust of its powerful engine shot the vehicle forward, and all four wheels were back on the road.

The driver managed to bring the car to a halt, and the two men climbed out. A quick examination showed that the left rear tire was flat. While the driver opened the trunk to pull out a spare, Mike got Ann and Brandon out of the car, then returned to offer a helping hand to the driver.

"You do your job, I'll do mine," he said.

The man's hostility was evident. "Okay, pal, if that's the way you want it," Mike said. "Just trying to be helpful."

"Then help the lady and stop acting like a bastard. She's been through a rough time."

"How would you know?" As soon as Mike said it, the truth hit him. "I get it. You're not *just* a chauffeur. It would be nice if the right hand knew what the left one was doing. But it does explain why you're packing that gun under your jacket."

"So you noticed."

"Not really. But usually when a guy has to change a tire in this weather, the first thing he'd do is take off his jacket and roll up his shirtsleeves. So I figured there was something under that jacket you don't want anyone to see. What are you, SAS?''

The man grinned. ''Took you long enough to figure it out, Yank.'' He offered his hand. ''Jeremy Hollingsworth.''

''Mike Bishop.''

''You CIA?''

''RATCOM.'' At Hollingsworth's questioning look, Mike added, ''Rescue and Anti-Terrorist.'' The two men shook hands.

Hollingsworth whistled. ''Special Ops! What in hell is a Special Ops man doing guarding a woman and kid? Isn't that what your police or FBI do?''

''Tell my boss that, will you? My team pulled Hamilton and the kid out of a tight spot. Now I'm supposed to be on leave like the rest of the team.''

At that moment a red Ferrari pulled up behind them. ''Figured he'd show up.''

Ricardo DeVilles hopped out of the car and came over to them. ''Is there a problem, Señor Bishop?'' he asked.

''No. We stopped so the kid could take a leak.''

''I do not find you amusing, *Señor*. My concern is for Ann.''

''At least we have that in common, DeVilles.''

''Is she all right?''

''Why wouldn't she be? Unless you know something that I don't.''

DeVilles hurried over to where Ann was standing with Brandon, who was clutching her around the waist.

''Ann, are you all right?''

''I'm fine, Ricardo.''

''What's wrong with Brandon?''

''The tire blew and it scared him. He'll be fine. Won't you, sweetheart?'' Brandon tightened his grip on her hand. ''Ricardo, I'm sorry, but I'm afraid I'll have to back out of our dinner plans. This whole day has been very hard on Brandon emotionally. Clayton's funeral and now this near accident. I don't want to leave him in the care of strangers. I hope you understand.''

DeVilles was the epitome of concern. "Yes, of course. But why can't he join us?''

"Do you mind, Ricardo?''

"Of course not, my dear. I'd be delighted.''

"Sweetheart, Ricardo has invited us out to dinner. Would you like that?''

He looked up fretfully. "Can Mike come, too?''

Way to go, kid! Mike leaned back against the car and folded his arms across his chest. He didn't want to miss a minute of this.

DeVilles looked at Ann. She threw a distraught glance at Mike. Then she bent down and told Brandon to go over to him. The kid came running over, and Mike winked at him and gave him a high five.

"Until the mystery of Clayton's death is resolved, Mr. Bishop is assigned to protect us,'' Ann informed DeVilles softly, out of the ear range of Brandon.

"Protect you? From whom?'' DeVilles asked.

"From the same people who murdered Clayton, Ricardo. It's a very long story.''

"Well then I suppose Señor Bishop will have to join us. This is not what I had in mind for tonight. Why don't you let me drive you back to your residency, though?''

Before she could reply, Mike opened the rear door of the limo as a sign they were ready to leave. Brandon climbed into the back seat.

"Oh, that's very kind of you, Ricardo, but that won't be necessary. I see they're through changing the tire.''

Mike noticed that DeVilles's mouth tweaked in displeasure. The guy was pissed. So DeVilles wasn't as smooth as he liked people to think.

"As you wish, Ann. I shall call for you at seven."

"We'll look forward to it. All of us," she added with a smile of amusement.

He clasped her hand and drew it to his lips. "Until then, my dear."

"Mike, do you love Ann?" Brandon asked later that evening, as the two of them watched her and DeVilles on the dance floor.

The kid had just launched an RPG at him. He'd always heard to be wary of anything that might come out of a child's mouth, but he never expected a rocket propelled grenade.

"Why would you think that, kid?"

"'Cause even though you yell at her a lot, sometimes you look at Ann like my daddy used to look at my mommy, and he always told me how much he loved her."

"My job is to protect her."

"You mean from those bad guys who were so mean to us in Kourou?"

"That's right, pal."

"Are they gonna come here after us?" He saw fright rising in the boy's eyes and was sorry he hadn't given the kid a more diplomatic answer.

"No way, pal. They wouldn't be that stupid."

"'Cause they're afraid of you and the other guys in your squad?"

"That's right."

"But the other guys in the squad aren't here with you."

"Well…ah…that's because my boss figures I can handle them alone."

"But there were a lot of the mean guys, Mike." The youngster's eyes sparkled with awe. "Wow, I bet you're the bravest guy in the whole world."

The kid was really beginning to grow on him. "Maybe

not the whole world, pal. But you can be sure I'm not going to let anything happen to Ann or you."

Mike swung his gaze back to the couple on the dance floor. They moved well together to the rhythm of the music. It was plain to see they'd danced together before.

Another thing that was plain to see was that DeVilles's interest in her was more than that of a family friend. That kiss he'd given her at the cemetery sure hadn't been casual! She seemed oblivious to his interest, though. Her body language neither encouraged nor discouraged his attentions, and she certainly didn't exhibit any of the unconscious mannerisms a woman often displays when she's flirting with a man.

But Mike's instincts told him that this DeVilles guy was bad news. Instinct was imperative in the business he was in. Instinct had often gotten him through some damn tight squeezes—and his instinct distrusted Ricardo DeVilles.

Why? Did the man present a danger to Ann...or did he resent DeVilles's personal interest in her?

The woman was screwing up his psyche. For the first time in his adult memory, Mike couldn't trust his instinct. *That* scared the hell out of him.

Chapter 11

The next day Mike accompanied Ann to the legal firm that was handling the reading of Clayton's will. Brandon remained at the State Department. Once again Jeremy Hollingsworth was their driver, which took some of the onus off Mike's shoulders. He knew now that in an emergency he'd have a backup, since he had his suspicions. Why would a tire blow at the same time a van almost drove them off the road?

"I'd like to check out that flat tire," he said to Jeremy, while they waited outside the lawyer's office.

"It's being done," Hollingsworth said. "And we've checked out the license number of the van. It had been reported stolen earlier that day, and has since been found abandoned."

"License number! When in hell did you have a chance to do that? You were pretty busy trying to keep the limo on the road."

"I memorized the number when it moved in on us."

Mike grinned. "Glad you're on board, Brit. Did you get any prints off the van?"

He shook his head. "Wiped clean. Could be whoever stole it was just being cautious."

"Or knew we'd try to trace fingerprints," Mike said. "Which means whomever it was knew their ID would pop up on police or Agency records, or they wouldn't have bothered to wipe down that van."

"Most likely," Jeremy said.

"My guess is that Ann's in as much danger here as she was in D.C. and French Guiana. What does SAS think?"

Jeremy snorted. "I wouldn't be playing chauffeur if they didn't think so."

"What bothers me is our two agencies have us protecting her, but who's trying to figure out who wants her dead?" Mike said.

Jeremy shrugged. "French Guiana, Washington and now London. Whoever it is has long arms."

"Or deep pockets," Mike said with a worried frown. He glanced impatiently at his watch. "How long does it take to read a damn will?"

For a long moment after the lawyer finished, Ann sat stunned. She finally found her voice. "What about my custody of Brandon?"

"As you can see, Miss Hamilton, there is no reference to that in the will. Other than bequeathing you his villa in the northern part of French Guiana, and donations to several charities, Mr. Burroughs's grandson is the beneficiary of the balance of the assets. Which are quite considerable. No reference is made regarding the child's custody."

This was too much. More than she could bear. Ann jumped to her feet. "Clayton added a codicil to his will. I saw it myself. I don't understand what's going on here.

Common sense would tell you that he would make a provision regarding Brandon's custody.''

"I'm sure he didn't expect to die so soon, Miss Hamilton.''

The condescending smirk on the lawyer's face was irritating. "Mr. Leonard, I suggest you contact Mr. Burroughs's lawyer in Kourou. Charles Breton drew up the codicil.''

"Unfortunately, Miss Hamilton, at this present time Mr. Breton is out of the country for the next several weeks. For years our firm has been retained by Mr. Breton to handle this type of business here when he is unable to attend himself. His secretary sent us a copy of the will,'' Leonard said in a patronizing tone.

"That is unfortunate, sir, but this is the twenty-first century, and we do have telephones, don't we, Mr. Leonard? I'm sure Mr. Breton's secretary knows where to reach him in an emergency.''

"I do not consider this an emergency, Miss Hamilton. It's simply a reading of a will. If there are any legal technicalities, they can be resolved upon Mr. Breton's return.''

"Well, I *do* consider this an emergency, sir. There is an unhappy little child who is literally being held prisoner by the British government. There is no doubt in my mind Charles Breton will be just as upset as I when he hears how Brandon is being hustled from pillar to post, and taken out of my custody for days—possibly even weeks. Especially considering Clayton Burroughs entrusted his grandson's safety to me on the day he was killed.''

"No doubt he would entrust the child's welfare to you, Miss Hamilton. I assume you were the child's nanny.''

"Your assumption is wrong, sir. I was Mr. Burroughs's executive assistant.''

A suggestive smirk appeared on Leonard's face. "Oh, I see.''

Ann stood up. She'd had enough of men pushing her around, mistaking grief for weakness. Friendship for intimacy. The time had come to make this condescending popinjay aware of it.

"No, you don't see, Mr. Leonard. Not at all! But that's inconsequential. I will expect you to contact Mr. Breton's office and get this matter resolved immediately. The sooner Brandon and I return to the United States, the happier we'll be. You can reach me through the British State Department. Good day, sir."

She was out the door before the astonished man could even get to his feet.

Mike had been around her enough to read her body language as soon as she came out of Leonard's office. He climbed in the back seat next to her. "So what's the problem?"

"Of all the supercilious…overbearing…*snobs.* That man wins the blue ribbon," she ranted. "When I told you I didn't hate men, I was wrong. I'm rescinding that statement."

"I take it you aren't referring to Clayton Burroughs."

She glared at him. "Of course not! I'm referring to that damn lawyer. It's no wonder people dislike them."

"Take a deep breath, Hamilton," he said. "What did he say to upset you?"

She turned her head and looked him in the eyes. "Bishop, why do men assume women are incapable of common sense?"

That question was a booby trap and Mrs. Bishop raised her son to believe if you step in horse manure you'll attract flies. She saved him from sidestepping the question and continued to vent. Between references to the lawyer's mental condition and the actual will, by the time she finished her tirade, Mike concluded that there was nothing in the will giving Ann custody of Brandon.

"Relax, Ann. You're killing the messenger. This Leonard's only a grunt."

"With an attitude!" she snapped.

"You can't blame him for what's in the will."

"You men are all alike. A big fraternal brotherhood of empty-headed, chest-pounding baboons."

Dammit! One sentence and the flies had begun buzzing around his head. He'd need a stick to clean the manure off his shoes.

"Ann," he said calmly, "forget Leonard. You know as well as I that you're really upset because of this setback over Brandon." He tried a grin. "If we put our heads together, we should be able to come up with a solution."

She eyed him sharply. "Are you patronizing me, Bishop?"

"Have I ever?"

She broke into a reluctant grin. "No, that's for sure."

"Good girl." He leaned back, relieved. He had just shaken the stuff off his shoes.

"Now *that's* patronizing, Bishop!" But this time her grin was genuine.

He couldn't help thinking she'd had enough stress in the last few days to last a lifetime. She was strung tightly and needed to relax.

"You need a change of pace, Hamilton. Let's play hooky for a couple hours."

"Hooky? Are you serious?"

"Sure. We'll stroll among the pigeons at Trafalgar Square, eat some fish and chips, drink a beer at a local pub. No abductors, assassins or custody hassles with uptight lawyers. For a couple hours we'll be Ann and Mike doing London. How about it?"

"I thought you said you never mix business and pleasure, Mike?" Even though she tried to appear reluctant, he could tell by the gleam in her eyes that the idea appealed to her.

"I won't charge the Agency for my time. Jeremy, stop the car."

The driver pulled over and Mike jumped out of the limo, then reached out and took Ann's hand and helped her out. Leaning down, he said to Hollingsworth, "Jeremy, you can leave. We'll get back on our own."

The agent gave him a disgruntled look, then said sotto voce to him, "Sure hope you know what you're doing, Yank."

After feeding the pigeons at Trafalgar Square, on impulse they took a tour bus that took them on an hour's tour of several points of interest including Buckingham Palace, the Parliament Building and the famous landmark Big Ben. Then they strolled along eating fish and chips, before ducking into a quaint pub to enjoy a cool brew.

As they sipped the beer, Ann said, "I really enjoyed this today, Mike. Thank you."

"So did I." Funny, he meant it. It was like the dinner they'd had together in Washington. Once she relaxed, Ann Hamilton was good company—besides being easy on the eyes.

"I wish Brandon had been with us. He would have enjoyed himself." Her smile slowly slipped into a worried frown. "I saw that codicil myself, Mike. Mr. Leonard obviously has an earlier version of the will. I have a copy of the codicil in my safe at home. If I could get back to Kourou, I—"

"Don't even think it," Mike declared. "Until the assassin is caught, it would be too dangerous for you to go back there."

"Who knows when that will be," she lamented.

She looked so depressed, his heart went out to her. "Look, Ann, in the meantime get this Leonard to file a petition giving you temporary custody of Brandon. Since the kid has no living relatives, and he wants to be with you, there shouldn't be a problem. Then, whenever they reach Burroughs's lawyer, he can straighten it all out.''

''I suppose you're right, but that, too, will take time. They'll have to do a background search to make certain there are no other relatives. And I suppose while they do, they'll boot me out. So I'll have to leave Brandon.''

''It will only be for a short time.'' Mike was about to order them another glass of beer when his cell phone went off.

As he reached for it, he gave Ann a disgusted look. ''Must be a wrong number. Who here would know my number?'' He turned away. ''What?'' he said, impatiently into the phone.

The caller didn't waste time identifying himself. He didn't have to.

''Get the hell out of there, now,'' Jeremy ordered. ''I just got a call. The lab found a bullet imbedded in that tire.''

''Where are you?'' Mike asked.

''Where do you think? Right outside.''

Mike hung up and threw some bills on the table. ''We have to go.''

''Is there a problem?'' she asked.

''I'll tell you about it later.'' He took her arm and hustled her outside. The black limo was parked at the curb.

''How did Jeremy know we were here?''

''He's been with us from the beginning,'' Mike said.

''You mean even when we took the tour?''

''Yeah. He was hanging back at a discreet distance, but I spotted him.''

''Why didn't you tell me?''

''The object was to get your mind off your problems.''

''Well at least it worked. Trouble is, they don't go away, they just keep getting worse.''

Mike nodded. Truer words were never spoken. She had no idea just how much worse.

As she had suspected, because of the will, Ann became a persona non grata. Trying to explain this to Brandon as she packed her bag to leave him was very difficult. He broke into tears when he heard they would be separated again.

''Sweetheart, once they reach Mr. Breton—you remember him, dear, he was your grandfather's lawyer—he can straighten it all out. In the meantime, I'll have the lawyer here petition the court to give me temporary custody of you until it is all resolved.''

Everything was too confusing and overwhelming to a six-year-old. Brandon had clung to her as she left and she shed silent tears all the way to the hotel where Mike was registered. He insisted upon connecting rooms for her protection, which only added to her discomfort. She found herself sitting on the edge of a bed and staring with a dazed gaze at the strange walls of yet another hotel room.

Recent events had made her life chaotic. Brandon's custody. Clayton's death. Men abducting her. Assassins trying to kill her. Mike Bishop. CIA. It all was as mind-boggling as it was horrifying. Racked with heartrending sobs, she buried her head in the pillow.

Her last thought before slipping into slumber was the realization that she couldn't remember the last time her life had been normal. This all had to be an out-of-body experience or some such catastrophe, because this couldn't be the life of Ann Susan Hamilton.

Chapter 12

Her eyes popped open when the hand clamped over her mouth. Mike was leaning over her and put a finger to his lips to warn her to be quiet.

How long would she play this nightmare over in her sleep?

But it wasn't a dream. It was happening again. She sat up and he took his hand away.

"Don't say anything, just listen and do what I say," he whispered. "Somebody's been moving around outside your door for several minutes."

She swung a frightened gaze to the door. The crack under it revealed a shifting shadow blocking out the hall light.

"Don't make a sound. Get out of bed and go into my room."

Grabbing her robe, she followed him. Once inside his room, Mike carefully closed and locked the connecting door.

"Now, as soon as I leave, bolt the door and don't open it to anyone but me. And only if I say it's okay. If I don't say that, call Security at once."

"What are you going to do, Mike?"

"I'm going out there."

"Why don't you just call Security?"

"Whoever it is would be out of here before anyone would show up. I want to have a private talk with whoever they are and find out who's behind this."

"You mean you think there's more than one?"

"I don't know. There was more than one person in that car that tried to run us off the road."

"I thought that was an accident?"

"Just do as I say." She gasped when she saw the pistol in his hand. It seemed to appear from nowhere. "You're going to have to move fast with that dead bolt, because I'll probably be spotted as soon as I open the door. If anything happens, call Security. And stay away from the door. If they've got assault weapons the door's no protection."

She forced the words past the lump that had suddenly formed in her throat. "Mike, this is too dangerous. Why don't you just wait for Security?"

"Just do what I say. Ready?"

She nodded.

Mike stepped out in the hallway, and the door clicked loudly as it swung closed. With a trembling hand, she slipped the dead bolt into place.

The man in the hallway spun around when he heard the door click shut. There were ten or twelve feet between the two doors, and the guy took off at a run. He ducked through the exit door when the ping of the elevator sounded and the doors swung open.

A security guard stepped out.

"Drop that gun, mate."

"I'll explain later. He's getting away," Mike said.

"Yeah, sure he is. Like there was someone else. I said drop it, bud."

Another ping sounded, another elevator door opened, and another security man showed up.

"Son of a bitch!" Mike mumbled, and laid the gun on the floor. "I can explain all this."

"Can't wait to hear it," the guard said, cuffing him.

"You don't understand. Someone was trying to break into our room."

"Yeah, sure there was. How do you Yanks say it, 'smile, you're on candid camera.'"

"Dammit, man, if you saw it all on camera, then you know it wasn't me."

"From the back, you all look alike."

"Really? So he was barefoot, barechested and wearing only jeans."

"I didn't notice," the guard said.

"Well, I did. He was bearded, had dark, shoulder-length hair, was wearing a black leather jacket, jeans and boots. And if you guys ever try using stairs instead of announcing your arrival on elevators, you would have run into him. How long have you guys been at this job?"

"Long enough to catch you, mate. You got any ID?"

"Not on me." Mike gave up. These guys were so thick-headed there was no reasoning with them. "My room's right down the hallway. And I have a witness to what happened." He strode away.

"Since I can't, do you mind knocking on the door?" Mike said, when they reached his room.

"Ann, open the door. It's okay."

Her eyes widened with surprise when she saw his hands cuffed behind his back and the two security guards.

"What's going on, Mike?" Ann asked.

"These guys think I'm the one who was trying to break into your room."

"What is your name, ma'am?" Thick Head asked.

"Ann Hamilton," she said.

"And you're acquainted with this man."

"Yes," Ann said. Her violet eyes were full of confusion when she glanced at Mike.

"Are you related to him?"

"No, I'm not. We are, ah…business acquaintances."

"What business are you in that you share connecting rooms with members of the opposite sex?"

Mike didn't like how the big mouth was talking to Ann. The guy was a dunce to mistake Ann for a hooker. If his hands weren't cuffed he'd punch the bastard right in the middle of that smirk on his ugly mug.

"Is that question germane to this particular problem, Officer?"

Way to go, baby! Thick Head had ruffled her feathers and she wasn't about to take any lip from him.

"He's not a police officer, Ann. He's merely a security guard," Mike said.

"You want to tell us what happened here?" the guard said.

"Mr. Bishop came into my room about fifteen minutes ago, woke me up, and told me someone in the hallway was trying to break into my room. We came into this room, he told me to lock the door when he leaves, and not to let anyone in."

"Did you see this individual who allegedly was trying to break into your room?"

"No, but I did see his shifting shadow in the crack between the floor and the door."

"And you said Bishop came into your room. What did you need connecting rooms for if the two of you weren't sharing a bed as you claim?"

"You have a problem with that, pal?" Mike said.

"Sounds more like you're the one with the problem." Thick Head and the other stooge broke into laughter.

"You two are a great act," Mike said. "When does Moe show up, or is it Curly? I never could keep track of who was who."

Luckily for him they didn't get it. Back home, a crack like that would probably have gotten him a punch in the gut. He reminded himself to keep his cool. "Look, my ID's in my wallet on the dresser. Check it out."

Thick Head looked through the wallet and pulled out the ID. Then he picked up the telephone and dialed the desk. After a mumbled conversation he looked up at Ann. "What did you say your last name was, lady?"

"Hamilton. Ann Hamilton."

What a detective! On top of the rest of his stupidity, the bastard must suffer with short memory loss. From the looks of that flattened nose he'd probably been a boxer who took one punch too many. Maybe he should cut him some slack.

After a few more grunts and mumbles into the telephone, the guard hung up. "Okay, you two, get dressed."

"How in hell am I supposed to get dressed with my hands cuffed behind my back?" Mike asked.

"Just don't try to get clever, mate." Thick Head nodded to his partner, and the guy unlocked the cuffs. "You must think we're stupid."

"Never entered my mind," Mike said.

"I figure you two are working this hotel and thought you'd get away with it. I'm turning you over to the police."

"One look at that tape, and they'll know it wasn't me," Mike said.

"Yeah, but it was you running down the hallway with a loaded gun, mate. We don't take kindly to that here. You

ain't over in the States now where you can get away with
that stuff.''

''And what are you charging *me* with?'' Ann said. ''I've
been in this room since I checked in.''

''Could be, lady. But you said you weren't related to
this guy, so how come you registered as his wife?''

''Wife!'' Ann threw Mike a scathing look. ''You registered me as your wife?''

Mike shrugged. ''Just protecting your reputation.''

Short of smoke coming out of her nose and ears, Ann
spun on her heel and went into her bedroom.

Thick Head followed her to the doorway. ''And keep
this door open, and don't try anything cute, cutie, or I'll
have to come in there and keep an eye on you.''

She slammed the door in his face.

How can he sleep? Ann asked herself as she glanced at
Mike sitting with his legs stretched out, ankles crossed,
arms folded across his chest and his eyes closed. For the
past hour they'd been cooped up at the police station in a
small, gray-walled room not much larger than a cloak-
room, and barren except for a table and two chairs. It
didn't even have a two-way mirror. She supposed it could
be worse; at least they weren't behind bars.

''How long can they keep us here?'' she said.

He opened his eyes. ''Relax, Ann. Once they check
those tapes, they'll know they were wrong and release us.''

''They said they're holding you because you were running down the hallway with a gun.''

''I have the right to protect us. Someone was trying to
break into your room. I'm sure the police aren't as stupid
as that punch-drunk security guard.''

''Well maybe if you would have changed your attitude
he'd have been more understanding.''

"I noticed you ran out of patience pretty quickly with him."

"What do you expect? The man literally accused me of being a prostitute."

"I rest my case." He closed his eyes again.

"How can you try to sleep at a time like this?"

He raised his lids. She could see irritation in those hazel eyes. "It would be easy if you'd relax and be quiet, Hamilton. Unlike you, I've yet to sleep tonight."

"I'm sorry. I'll be quiet."

She began to pace back and forth. He opened his eyes and sat up. "Okay, what's the problem, Hamilton?"

"Problem? What problem could I possibly have? My best friend was murdered, someone is apparently trying to do the same to me, I'm having difficulty getting custody of Brandon, and I've been arrested as a suspected hooker and confined in this little box of a room with a…a…"

"A what, Hamilton?"

"Oh, forget it." She resumed her pacing.

He leaped to his feet and grasped her by the shoulders. The latent anger he was trying to conceal was apparent at this close proximity.

"A what, Hamilton?" he repeated. "I don't like this arrangement any more than you do. My job is Special Ops, not wet-nursing temperamental females who don't have enough sense to recognize when someone is trying to help them."

His face was so close she could feel the warmth of his breath. There was an escalating excitement in being this close to Mike Bishop that had nothing to do with fright. She knew he wouldn't hurt her. It was the male essence of the man that her femininity responded to immediately.

She sensed he felt a similar reaction, because for the briefest instant of a drawn breath he paused. She parted her lips and he lowered his head. Just as they were about to kiss, the door opened.

"Is this kiss-and-make-up time?"

They stepped apart and stared at Jeremy Hollingsworth. "What are you doing here?" Mike asked.

"The police called the State Department. I happened to have been around when the call came in."

"Why would the police call them? Ann's not a British subject."

"Oh, I bet I'm to blame. I told them to," Ann said.

"Dammit, Ann, you should have kept them out of this. I told you once the police looked at those security films, we'd be off the hook."

"I guess I wasn't thinking."

"Sorry, Hollingsworth. Hope it hasn't blown your cover."

"His cover? What does that mean?" Ann asked. She swung her gaze to the agent. "Don't tell me you're in the CIA, too."

"No, Miss Hamilton. I am not in the CIA. Anyway, you're free to leave. Shall we get out of here."

They stopped at the desk, reclaimed their personal items, and it was close to sunrise by the time Jeremy drove them back to the hotel.

Larry and Moe were in the lobby. Still no sign of Curly. The two guards glared at them when they stepped into the elevator and as the doors closed Mike couldn't resist flipping them the finger.

"Do you actually take pleasure in resorting to that immature, obscene gesture?" Ann asked, disgusted.

"Lady, you have no idea," Mike said. He grinned all the way up to his room.

After checking Ann's room, he put the Do Not Disturb

sign on the door handles, and then went to bed. He fell asleep as soon as his head hit the pillow knowing, beyond the shadow of a doubt, the security camera on the floor would get a lot of attention while he slept.

Chapter 13

Ann had too much on her mind to get back to sleep. She had slept enough before the incident to make any further attempt an impossibility. In truth, she didn't know what to make of tonight's episode. It could have been a hotel thief trying to rob the room, and naturally he'd run if someone popped out of a door holding a gun.

On the other hand, since Clayton's death there had been so many disturbing occurrences that she'd be naive to believe they were just coincidences. The attack in French Guiana certainly was intentional, but not necessarily related to Clayton's death—even if the CIA thought the contrary; the incident in the dressing room in D.C. was questionable—Mike seemed certain that someone had entered the room after she did; the attack near the Ellipsis could have been a question of being in the wrong place at the wrong time; the accident with the tire and now this incident in the hotel... She shot to her feet and began to pace back and forth. Coincidence?

Undoubtedly Mike was right: someone believed she knew something that could reveal the identity of the person responsible for Clayton's death. And if it hadn't been for Mike, she might very well have fallen victim to the same fate as Clayton.

But as hard as she tried, she couldn't think of one incident or conversation in Kourou that would even hint at a possible murderer.

She'd been intimidated in one way or another since the day Clayton was killed. On the other hand, these close calls had happened in French Guiana, D.C. and now London. It was hard to believe that whoever was responsible had accomplices in all these countries.

Ann sat down on the edge of the bed. She had to take charge of her life again. But how could she if she believed she was a target of some assailant? It could take months to track down the killer or killers, and she couldn't remain under Mike's protection all that time, any more than she could afford to remain unemployed. Most certainly she was out of a job. Besides which, with Clayton gone she had no further desire to live in French Guiana.

In the meantime she had to find a means of support. A CIA green light or not, she'd have to go back to Kourou to pack up her belongings. Charles Breton could handle the disposing of the real estate: her condo, Clayton's mountain villa he bequeathed to her and his house in Kourou that would be Brandon's. She intended to raise him in the United States.

But at the moment her greatest problem to resolve was employment. And if she were going job hunting, her best bet would be to return to the profession in which she was skilled—fashion photography. At the time she quit, Barney had told her if she ever wanted to return, her old job would be waiting. The question of Brandon's custody should be cleared up as soon as they located Charles Breton, so it shouldn't be a problem to return to the United States. As for the attempts on her life—if they were actual attempts—it wasn't any more dangerous in the States than anywhere else.

Ann reached for the telephone.

"Hello." There was an edge of sleepiness to the greeting combined with the gruffness. Nevertheless her heart swelled with pleasure at the sound of the familiar voice.

"Barney, this is Ann."

"Annie!" The grumpiness quickly changed to concern. "What's wrong, baby?"

"I need a job, Barney."

"A job? You wake me up at midnight to ask for a job! As much as I love you, Annie, you know I'm an early to bed, early to rise guy. Couldn't this have waited until morning?"

"I'm sorry, Barney. I forgot about the time difference."

"So what happened, Burroughs give you the sack?"

"Clayton is dead, Barney. Murdered."

There was a long silence on the other end, then Barney said. "Geez, honey, I'm sorry. I'll come down to give you some moral support."

"I'm not in Kourou, Barney. I'm in London. Clayton was interred here the day before yesterday. I'm waiting to settle the custody of Brandon, and then I expect to return to the States."

"And how is the youngster doing? Didn't you tell me Burroughs was his last remaining relative?"

"He's holding up very well. Clayton made me his legal guardian and I hope to adopt him. I love him so much, Barney."

"You said Burroughs was murdered. Was it a robbery?"

"No. It's very involved, Barney. I'll explain it all to you when I see you. Question is, can you use me?"

"You bet I can, Annie. There's a shoot scheduled here for the beginning of the week that's right up your alley. Can you make it?"

"I'll know shortly. There's a legal delay here, and as soon as we reach Clayton's lawyer, I'll be able to straighten it out. I'd hate to leave London without Brandon, right now he's under the protection of the British State Department."

"Isn't that unusual?"

"Everything about this whole affair is unusual, Barney." She glanced up when Mike tapped on the connecting door and came into the room. "As I said, I'll explain it all to you when I see you. I'll get back to you as soon as I can. And, thanks, Barney. I love you."

She hung up and looked at Mike. "Bishop, do you ever wait to be *invited* into a room?"

"I knocked, didn't I? How about breakfast?"

He was clean-shaven, water still glistened on his hair from a shower, and he looked as if he'd slept for about eight hours, instead of three. How did the man do it?

"I'm surprised to see you up. You didn't sleep very long."

"I'm used to that. What about it? Are you hungry?"

Ann nodded. "Give me a minute to freshen up."

Mike plopped down in the chair. "So was that your ex-boss you were speaking to?" he asked, as she quickly ran a brush through her hair.

"Yes. We've always stayed in touch." *He has a mind like a steel trap. I should have told him no just to deflate his ego.*

Ann powdered her face and lightly brushed on some lip gloss. As she leaned closer to check the final results, she caught his reflection in the mirror. His gaze was fixed on her, and he looked pensive.

What was he thinking? He was such a private person, as enigmatic at times as he was challenging at others. But whatever, he was the most infuriating, frustrating individual she'd ever known—and the most fascinating and exciting to be around. A woman would have to be out of her mind to ever fall in love with him, but she suspected it would be a heck of a ride while it lasted.

Cool it, Ann. You've been too long without a man. Mike Bishop is starting to look better and better to you.

Since leaving the States she hadn't missed being intimately involved with a man. Not that she'd ever been inordinately promiscuous. She'd never even considered Ricardo DeVilles, despite his obvious interest in her.

But now, since Mike Bishop entered your life, you're suddenly asking yourself, when was the last time you "got laid"? Isn't that how you put it, Bishop? You're such a bad influence!

Lucky for her he didn't believe in mixing business with pleasure, because that Stockholm Syndrome was chipping away at her resistance.

Grinning at her own train of thought, she turned away from the mirror and met the full force of a wide grin on that rugged face of his. On top of everything else was Bishop a mind reader?

They decided to eat breakfast right in the hotel's coffee shop. Sitting across a table eating with him was becoming a habit.

"Tell me, Mike, how can you *guard* me and eat at the same time?"

"You'd be surprised. I bet you didn't know that I can walk and whistle at the same time, too."

"You mean while you're eating and guarding me?"

They both broke into laughter, and suddenly they were merely two people enjoying breakfast together.

"Seriously, Mike, in movies the bodyguard is always standing silently scanning the room."

"So what do you want to know about this room?" he asked, without turning around to look. "There are five tables, including ours, being served. The doors to the kitchen are on the right side of the room. The cashier's in her fifties, about five-four. The waitress is about five-six, red hair, and weighs about 120. There are two men at the corner table, both are wearing black suits. The dark-haired one is wearing a blue shirt and a blue-and-gray tie, the gray-haired one a white shirt with a maroon tie. There are a woman and two small children at the table next to them. A just-married couple at the table in the opposite corner, and—"

"How do you know they're newlyweds?" she asked.

"It's easy to tell newlyweds—they always look like they're doing something illicit. The elderly woman at another table is wearing a black hat with a large red rose, and there's a man reading a newspaper at the table nearest the door. He's the one I'm most concerned about."

"Why him?" she asked.

"Because he came in and sat down after we did. Took a table nearest the door when most people in a restaurant try to avoid that high traffic area. And he only ordered a cup of coffee."

"Maybe he's eaten breakfast already."

"Maybe he has."

"So why aren't you concerned about the two men in black suits?"

"If they were up to no good, they wouldn't have backed themselves into a corner."

"Okay, why not the lone woman? A woman could be a cold-blooded killer."

"True, but if she'd intended to be trouble, she'd want to appear nondescript. That big red rose she's wearing calls attention to her."

"Is this all part of your Special Ops training?" she asked.

"We're trained to be observant, but I learned a lot from my father. He worked for the CIA."

"Is that why you joined it?"

"It was an easy sell. I was a Navy SEAL, and they recruited me into the Agency."

"Where are you from, Mike?"

"I was born in Milwaukee."

"Ever been in love?"

To her surprise he looked uncomfortable. "Sure. I love a lot of things."

"You know what I mean."

"No. Guess I just never had the time to fall in love. College, then Afghanistan and Iraq. Wouldn't want to mess up some gal's life—or change mine. I like what I do."

"Living on the edge."

"Guess you could say that."

"Well, if living on the edge is anything like what I've gone through this past week, you can have it. Nice and easy is my style. The only excitement I need is in bed."

Shocked, she brought her hand to her mouth.

Good Lord! How could I have said that? She was too embarrassed to look at him. *Get your mind off of sex, Ann!*

Fortunately, before she dropped dead from mortification, his cell phone went off, sparing her his response to her outrageous remark.

The last thing Mike ever expected to hear from Ann's mouth was her last statement. He was on the verge of pursuing the remark when his damn cell phone went off.

If he hadn't been waiting for Baker's call, he'd have ignored it.

Avery Waterman was the caller.

"I'm returning your call to Baker, Mike," Waterman
said. "He's out of the office. What's the problem?"

"I need the Agency to do a background check on a
Charles Breton. B-R-E-T-O-N. He's a lawyer in Kourou,
French Guiana."

"I gather this is related to the Burroughs case?"

"Yeah. He's Burroughs's lawyer. There's a legal hang-
up over Brandon Burroughs's custody, and Breton is the
lawyer who drew up the codicil making Hamilton the legal
guardian of the kid."

"So why are you interested in this guy's background?"

"Because the will was read yesterday, and the codicil
wasn't attached. Now it seems Breton's out of the country
and can't be reached. Check him out and see what turns
up."

"You said he's out of the country. Do you know
where?"

"No. That's the big mystery. He went off on his boat
somewhere."

"How are things going with Miss Hamilton?"

"Not good." Mike glanced at Ann. "There's been another attempt on her life." He saw her head jerk up in
shock. "I'll tell you all about it when I return."

"When will that be?"

"Can't say for sure. Right now we're held up here because of that custody delay, or we would have been on
our way home by now."

"Okay," Waterman said. "We'll get on this Breton
business and get back to you."

As soon as he hung up, Ann said, "What attempt on
my life? Aren't you jumping to conclusions? That man in

the hotel might just have been trying to burglarize the room.''

"I doubt it. Regardless, the limo accident was deliberate. The van had been stolen and…'' He decided it would be better not to mention the bullet in the tire.

A shocked gasp was evidence of her distress as the reality set in. "We all could have been killed." She cradled her head in her hand. "Oh, Mike, what is this all about, that whoever's behind it is even willing to kill an innocent six-year-old child?''

"That's what we're going to find out," he said. "Trust me, Ann, and you can take that to the bank.''

She dropped her arm and looked at him. "Speaking of the bank, Mike, I've decided to return to my old job as a fashion photographer. With Clayton gone I certainly have no further desire to work for the Space Consortium. I hope to settle in New York and get some permanence in my life again. Once I can go back to Kourou, I'll pack up my things and stop living out of a suitcase.''

"New York! Apparently that permanence doesn't include peace and quiet.''

"That's where the action is and most of the shoots. With a young child to raise, I don't intend to accept any overseas assignments.''

"Can you be that selective?''

"I think so. Barney has a couple of photographers that will jump at the chance to do overseas shoots, so I don't expect too much opposition.'' She glanced at the clock. "I'd like to go and visit Brandon now.''

"Sure," he said, and reached for the check.

Once outside, the doorman hailed a cab for them. "I see our breakfast friend finished reading the newspaper,'' Mike said as they pulled away. Ann glanced out the window in time to see the man step out of the revolving door of the hotel.

On the way she borrowed Mike's cell phone and called Leonard. The attorney informed her that thus far they'd been unsuccessful in contacting Charles Breton, and Brandon would have to continue to remain in England. It was devastating news, and she'd now have to tell Brandon the disappointing setback.

As soon as he saw her, Brandon ran into Ann's arms. "I'm tired of this place, Ann. I want to go with you and Mike."

"You will, sweetheart, as soon as Mr. Breton clears it all up."

"When will that be?" Brandon whined. "I don't like this place. I want to be with you guys."

Ann hugged him. "I know you do, sweetheart, and we're doing everything we can to hurry it up." She stepped back and smiled at him. "Guess what I'm going to do?"

"What?" he asked. With a balled fist he rubbed the tears from his eyes.

"I'm going back to the old job I had before I worked for your grandfather."

"You mean taking pictures?"

"Yes, sweetheart. How would you like to live in New York?"

He shrugged. "I don't know. Is it like Kourou?"

"Not really, dear. It's a very large city with tall skyscrapers—and lots of fun things to do. That's where I'll be working."

"Who'll take care of me while you're working?"

"We'll find you a nice nanny. And don't forget, in the fall you'll be old enough to start school. I thought while we're waiting to hear from Mr. Breton, I'd fly back there, find us a nice place to live, and start interviewing nannies."

"You mean you're going away?" His lower lip started to quiver.

"Only for a few days, darling. And I'll call you twice a day." She hugged him again. "I couldn't bear to be away from you any longer than that."

Mike had sat by in silence and clamped his jaw shut during the conversation. When they finally left two hours later Mike was near to bursting. He opened up in a torrent.

"No way, Hamilton!"

"What are you talking about?"

"Going back to New York."

"I told you all about it," she declared.

"You never said you meant right away. It's too dangerous right now."

"It can't be any more dangerous in New York than here, or Washington and French Guiana. I'm a working girl, Mike. Remember? I can't afford to sit around idle for an indefinite length of time."

He could see the logic to her argument, but someone was determined to kill her, and the only way she could remain safe was to keep her sequestered under guard until the CIA got to the bottom of who killed Burroughs.

"Why don't you give this another week, Ann, or at least until the custody situation is resolved."

"I can't remain holed up in a hotel room for another week and let out of my cell just for meals. In another week I can find a place to live so that I can bring Brandon back to something other than a hotel room. Will you stop and think how that child's been shuffled around since all this began?"

"I don't deny it's been tough on the kid, but it would be a damn sight tougher if he loses you, too, Ann."

"Mike, what if I told you I don't believe anything will happen to me as long as you're with me?"

Her confession took him by surprise. For a long moment

he looked deeply into those violet eyes of hers. The trust in them wrenched at his heart. It wasn't fair. It was fighting dirty. You stand up and duke it out, not sneak into a man's conscience with a pair of violet eyes that could haunt a guy for life.

"Ann, you need better protection than I can give you. I'm in Special Ops, and protecting you is a job for people who are trained for that kind of duty."

"I understand, and for now, all I'm asking is for your cooperation. Please, Mike."

Every fiber of his being warned him to refuse. He had the common sense to realize this even if she didn't.

But she had the violet eyes.

"One condition."

"Anything, Mike," she said, a restored hope gleaming in those two weapons of destruction.

"A complete truce between us. No more tantrums or going off on your own. You have to promise to do everything I tell you to do."

"I promise, Mike."

"Well, I've got some calls to make before I can agree."

As soon as they got back to the hotel, Mike put in calls to the guys in the squad. He was able to reach all of them by the time he took Ann to dinner that evening.

"Okay, this is the deal," he told her. "I called in the squad. They're off duty, but doing this as a personal favor to me. For the next week you'll be guarded 24/7. Got that?"

"You mean even at night?" she groaned.

"It's all or nothing at all, Ann. Decide now, because that's the only way I'll agree to this. I figure within the week you'll get custody of Brandon. I talked to Rick Williams and Pete Bledsoe. They'll take Brandon back to the States when the time comes, and that will save you the trouble of coming back here. If we do this, you've got to promise to abide by the rules.''

''I promise, Mike.'' Those violet eyes were misting with tears.

''Okay, we'll go back tomorrow.'' He tried to steel himself against the draw of those eyes. ''You want to take in a movie?''

''If you want to, Mike.''

Right answer.

Chapter 14

Dave Cassidy, Kurt Bolen and Don Fraser met them at the airport when they landed.

"So where do we stand?" Mike asked, after an exchange of greetings and handshakes.

"My sister and brother-in-law are letting us use their condo," Dave said. "They'll be out of the country for the next month."

"Good."

"Where are Bledsoe and Williams?" Cassidy asked.

"I contacted them and told them to stay in England until Ann gets official custody of the kid and then brings him back. Let's go to that apartment and get settled in. Then we'll work out a schedule."

The apartment was on the thirty-fourth floor of an exclusive high-rise hotel in Manhattan. Each condo unit took up an entire floor, and only a programmed floor key card could stop the elevator on the requested floor.

As they looked around in awe at the elegant apartment with its ten-foot-high ceilings, marble columns and crystal chandeliers, Kurt Bolen whistled softly, "Cassidy, what in hell does your brother-in-law do for a living?"

"He's a Frenchman. Owns some kind of financial consulting firm," Dave said.

"And a drug cartel on the side to afford all this," Don Fraser added.

"Naw, you know my sister's Kim Barrington."

"The movie actress?" Ann asked.

Cassidy nodded. "Have you seen any of the movies she's in?"

"Who hasn't?" Mike said. "We watched one on the plane coming back."

"Too bad she got all the looks in the family, Cassidy," Bolen said, moving in to inspect more of the apartment.

"Maybe we should take our shoes off so we don't dirty that white carpet," Fraser said.

"Yeah, and we need a map to figure out the traffic pattern in here," Bolen grumbled. "With all these mirrored doors and walls, a person could get lost."

"Then I suggest we all learn it fast, starting now," Mike said.

A few minutes later, after checking out the apartment, they all sat down at the kitchen table.

"Okay, here's how I see it," Mike said. "There are twelve rooms and five bathrooms. That's a lot of rooms to cover. But the good news is that we don't have to worry about windows, and the main door and a kitchen door are the only access in or out of the apartment.

"Now, there are only two ways on or off this floor— the elevator or the locked door to the stairway. Since a key card programmed for this floor only is needed to open either one, we'll post a man in the hall lounge right outside the main door here, giving him a full view of the elevator, stairway and the two doors. Do you all read me?''

When they nodded, Mike continued. ''All right, there are four bedrooms—a master, two guests and one off the kitchen, probably intended for a servant. Apparently, there is no live-in servant since there are no personal effects in that room. We'll close and lock up the master bedroom— that's out of bounds for all of us. Ann takes one of the guest bedrooms and that leaves two for us.

''Two men will work twelve-hour shifts, eight to eight, with a man in the hall lounge and one inside here. That puts two of us awake at all times. Fraser and Bolen take the first watch at 20 hundred. At O200 switch posts. Then tomorrow morning at 0800 Cassidy and I will relieve you. Any questions?''

''I have one,'' Ann said. ''There is no standard time when I have to do a shoot. It can be morning, afternoon or evening. What does that do to your schedule?''

''The schedule is to indicate who's officially on watch at a given time. When you're out of this apartment, Ann, at least the two awake men on watch will be covering you for sure, and most likely more of us. I've never seen one of these guys sleep for twelve straight hours.

''Frankly, I'd prefer to keep you confined to this apartment, so whenever possible, try to keep our schedules in mind. It will make it easier on all of us for the next week.''

''I can't tell you how grateful I am to all of you,'' Ann said. ''I know you guys are giving up your free time to do this, and I wish I knew a way of making it up to you.''

''Just do as we ask, Ann. It'll make it easier on all of us.''

She looked at Mike. He could separate business and pleasure so easily. Last night they had shared a pleasant dinner together and then went to a movie as if they didn't have a care in the world. Today it was all business again, and he was in charge.

Well, he seemed to know what he was doing, and she had promised him to cooperate to get him to agree to this, so she wasn't going to give him any arguments.

"If you'll excuse me, I think I'll get settled in. Which bedroom do you want me to take?"

"One of the bathrooms has a bathtub and shower stall. The other two have only showers. I figure you might like a tub."

"You're right about that. I love hot baths," she said.

"Then it's yours." He pointed to one of the archways opening off the mammoth living room. "Through there and it's the second door on the right."

How does he remember all these details? she pondered in awe as she followed his directions to the designated room.

Ann sank down on the edge of the bed. Yesterday she was in London. Today she was here in New York in the luxury apartment of total strangers. What happened to her life? She sighed deeply and looked around her. The ivory and pale-yellow bedroom had a serene ambiance that was like a soothing balm to her frayed nerves—nerves that had been stretched almost to snapping with the alarming events and setbacks of the past week.

Wearily Ann got up, and after unpacking she drew a hot bath. Lowering herself into the mammoth tub, she leaned her head back against the rim and closed her eyes. Streams of warm water from jet sprays washed over her tired body with the effectiveness of a relaxing sedative. For some inexplicable reason—perhaps from the jet sprays, perhaps the effects of the room's serenity, or perhaps mere exhaustion from the treadmill she'd been on lately—she began to feel lethargic and her mind flooded with an inner peace. Somehow, no matter how grim everything seemed at the moment, she sensed it would all work out in the end. Maybe the world wasn't so bad after all. Like Browning said, "God's in His Heaven..." And Mike Bishop's in charge down here.

After a phone call to Brandon, which diminished some of the upbeat attitude she'd achieved, Ann and her four-man escort went grocery shopping. It became an experience she'd never forget. The different types of food the fellows picked out to eat were as diversified as their personalities. It appeared that beer, pretzels and coffee were the only unanimous choices among the four of them.

Dave Cassidy broiled steaks for the evening meal, Mike made French-fried potatoes and Ann tossed a green salad. The fellows drank beer with their dinner, and she drank iced tea. She gave half of her steak to Mike and as much as she enjoyed the banter of the guys, she couldn't shake off the effects of her conversation with Brandon.

At eight o'clock when Don went out into the hall to start his watch, Ann turned down an invitation to watch the latest Kim Barrington film on DVD and retired to her room.

She called Barney on Mike's cell phone and arranged to meet him for lunch the following day. Then, after paging through several magazines she'd found in the den, she finally turned off the light and tried to sleep. But to no avail. She had a heavy heart. She missed Brandon and he'd sounded so sad and desolate on the telephone that it preyed on her.

Somewhere in the apartment a clock chimed one o'clock and she got out of bed, pulled on her robe, and opened the bedroom door. Peering out, the hallway was dark. Moonlight gleaming through floor to ceiling windows cast silver rays across the marbled floor of the living room. The faint drone of the television in the den was a comforting sound in this unfamiliar apartment. Should she go in and join Don Fraser, or was it Kurt Bolen now?

No doubt at this late hour the other two men would be asleep. She couldn't help but wonder which bedroom Mike was in. But what difference did it make, anyway.

A light breeze carrying the sweet fragrance of roses drew her to the open doors of the terrace. She stepped outside and moved to the bricked railing. The view was breathtaking. Ann closed her eyes and lifted her face to catch the breeze as it feathered her hair.

"Can't you sleep?"

Startled she turned. Mike Bishop rose from a chair in a darkened corner.

"I could ask you the same thing. I thought this was your sleeping time."

"I was just considering going to bed." He moved closer, narrowing the gap that separated them, then leaned back against the wall.

"What a view," she murmured. "I bet you could reach up and pluck a star out of the sky."

"It would be easier to just pick one out of your eyes," he said.

The sensual huskiness in his voice sent a shiver down her spine. Her heartbeat quickened, and she turned her head and gazed out at the New York skyline to avoid looking into those wounded-deer hazel eyes of his. She could feel his stare fixed on her face.

She was scared of him. Scared of the effect he had on her. She reacted to his nearness like a teenage groupie to a rock star.

Like now. Her legs were trembling, her heart pounding, and she wanted him to kiss her. Recalling the excitement of the kiss he gave her in D.C., she yearned for him to kiss her again—now, like two lovers, with a starry sky twinkling overhead and the scent of roses permeating the air.

Romantic? Yes! She needed some romance in her life. Hearts and flowers. Dancing in the dark. Stolen kisses. Tender words of love.

It had been a long time since she'd thought about being in love—or having a man make love to her. She thought in this case it must be the latter. Yet, somehow it was hard to conjure up the image of Mike Bishop being romantic. While on the other hand if it came to hot sex—his was the only image she could visualize.

"So what's on your mind, Ann?"

She felt the heat of the blush that coursed through her.

"What do you mean?" she asked, too embarrassed to look him in the eye. With his powers of observation she'd crumble before him. If only he'd stop staring at her!

"Why can't you sleep? You're safe. We won't let anything happen to you."

"It's not that, Mike. It's Brandon. He wants me to come back to London."

"Did Leonard have any luck reaching Burroughs's lawyer?"

"No."

"I never should have left London, Mike. Another week one way or the other wouldn't make that much difference. Because I came back today, Barney wants me to start right away. I had hopes of finding a nice little house for Brandon and me first."

"If I were you, I'd forget both things, and after my squad leaves remain under protective care until this whole mess is resolved."

She finally turned her head and looked him in the eyes. "You didn't have much of a vacation, did you? And it's entirely my fault. I've spoiled it for the other guys, too, but at least they had a little time to... I mean a chance to…probably get together with their girlfriends or… I mean you were stuck with me the whole time.'' Her mind was back on sex again and she was rambling like a flustered virgin.

Mike chuckled. ''If I didn't know better, Hamilton, I'd swear you were hitting on me.''

''Hitting on you!'' She must have turned six shades of red. ''I'm sorry, it probably does sound like that, but that's not what I meant. We both agreed not to mix business and pleasure. To keep it strictly business between us.'' She moved away quickly. ''Well, I guess I'll make another attempt at sleeping. Good night, Mike.''

''Ann.'' She stopped and turned around. ''Yeah, that was our agreement. But I'll warn you now, lady, when this business is cleared up, I'll be coming after you.''

''What do you mean?''

''We've got a lot of lost pleasure time to make up.''

''You're pretty sure of yourself, Mike. Do you actually think I'm stupid enough to get involved with a guy who lives on the edge like you do?''

''I think it's out of both of our hands. Right now I want to pick you up and carry you to bed. Are you really going to deny you don't want me to? No, sweetheart, it won't fly. Those violet eyes tell me all I have to know. I figure it's going to be worth the wait.''

''I'm not denying the idea momentarily crossed my mind. Moonlight can put a lot of crazy ideas in a woman's head, but in the bright light of day, she faces reality. I want a husband who comes home to Brandon and me each night and not one who's in some godforsaken place on some kind of covert mission.''

''I don't remember whistling the 'Wedding March,' lady. I'm talking about a week in bed of nothing but hot sex.''

''Won't happen, Bishop. You don't *have* a brain or you

wouldn't be doing what you do for a living. Me, I have to put mine to a better use.''

''Pity,'' he said. Even with the distance between them she didn't have to see his face clearly to know he was smirking.

''What?''

''How afraid you are of a man.''

The arrogance of the man was maddening. ''You know, Mike, I'm grateful to you. A few minutes ago, mesmerized by a romantic moment, the idea of going to bed with you was very tempting. Thank you for reminding me of the danger in substituting moonlight for the real light of day.''

Chapter 15

Mike slept until seven and then got up and showered. Last night he'd gone to bed and lain thinking about Ann until jet lag kicked in. When he went into the kitchen Ann and Don Fraser were sitting at the breakfast table. Dave Cassidy joined them a few minutes later, since he was due to take the hall watch at eight.

As soon as Cassidy relieved Kurt Bolen, he came in and joined them. For the next hour they sat around talking and relaxing.

The men in the squad got along well with each other. There were no ego or personality clashes between them. No vying for authority. Mike was their undisputed leader. They accepted his judgment without a word of contradiction. Mike figured it was because each one was a specialist in a particular field, and knew he'd never doubt their individual ability when it was called for.

Since he'd forbidden anyone to use the telephones in the apartment, Ann borrowed his cell phone to call Brandon. Her eyes were misting when she hung up.

"How's the kid doing?" Mike asked.

"He's so sad. It breaks my heart to hear him. If only someone could locate Charles Breton."

"I'll see if the Agency's had any luck," Mike said, reaching for his cell phone.

"Where the hell are you, Bishop?" Avery Waterman ranted as soon as he picked up the phone. "You working for us or moonlighting? The hotel in London said you checked out yesterday, and I've tried to reach you a dozen times on your cell phone. I either get a busy signal or you don't answer. Don't you check your messages?"

"I had to charge the battery. It's working now."

"You are expected to check in daily."

"I'm supposed to be on leave, too? And you're supposed to be in Intelligence. You could have called the British State Department. Miss Hamilton informed them of her intentions. So chill out," Mike said.

Despite the irritation in Waterman's voice, Mike visualized his superior sitting behind his desk without a hair out of place or a wrinkle in his suit jacket. "We're in New York."

"New York!"

"Yeah. Miss Hamilton got her photography job back, and she'll be working here."

"Is the Burroughs lad with her?"

"No. He's still in London. Did you check out Charles Breton?"

"He's squeaky clean."

"That alone is suspicious. Have you ever met a lawyer who's squeaky clean? Any progress in locating Breton?"

"The chap appears to have disappeared into thin air. There's been no word from him since he left Kourou on the same day as Burroughs was murdered."

"Well, his secretary must have an idea where he was headed."

''She claims not. Breton said he'd contact her every other day. He hasn't done it. There have been no sightings of his boat since he left the harbor. We've alerted several coast guards, but they haven't seen him either.''

''Could be he's the one who whacked Burroughs, or met the same fate as Burroughs did.''

''That's possible, or his radio could be out of order. We'll keep following through on this end.''

''Hamilton clearly needs protection. Someone's going to have to take over here when I leave. Who have you got working on this case? There's sure been enough time to come up with something.''

''They're experienced agents and know their job.''

''Well obviously whoever's behind the murder believes that Hamilton knows something. I've been with her practically nonstop since the rescue. If she knows anything, she sure has me fooled.''

''Bishop, the point is she doesn't realize she knows something important. It'll come to her one of these days. Do you ever discuss the case with her?''

''Only the attempts on her life. She wants nothing more to do with the Space Consortium, and once she goes back to Kourou and packs up, she intends to return to the States, settle down with the kid and resume her career.''

''Where are you staying in New York?''

''In a borrowed apartment. It's secure.''

''What's the address?''

''I don't know. It's in Manhattan.''

''Well, I want to hear from you every day, is that clear?''

''Yeah, yeah. When's Prince Charming due back?''

''Same time you are.''

''Okay. Call me if you hear anything further on Breton.''

Mike hung up and went back and joined the others. Ann

looked up hopefully and he shook his head in answer to her unspoken question. "Nothing. No sign of him."

"You figure someone whacked the lawyer the same as Burroughs?" Bolen asked.

"Can't say. Could be wherever he is a cell phone might be worthless, but it seems odd that if his radio isn't working he wouldn't put into port somewhere and call."

"A lot can go wrong on a boat," Fraser said. "He could have had an accident or a fire."

"According to Waterman he's alerted several coast guards in surrounding countries. There's been no report of any fire or debris in the water. Trouble is without knowing where he was headed no one knows where to start looking."

"You mean it's like looking for a needle in a haystack," Ann said.

"Close," Mike said, "except a haystack is stationary which is a start at least."

"Baker got any theories?" Kurt asked. "He's got the brain for this kind of situation."

"He's on leave and not due back until we are."

Mike sat back and observed the two men and Ann together. This was the first time the Dwarf Squad had gotten this close to anyone they rescued. In the past as soon as they'd returned from a rescue mission, he and the rest of the squad would no longer be involved with that individual.

He knew Cassidy well enough to recognize that his second in command liked Ann. So did Williams and Bledsoe. There had been a lot of bonding between them.

Seems like he was the only one whoever had a cross word with her. They'd clashed from the time they met. Chemistry? The chemistry between him and Ann was boiling over. Last night it took every particle of willpower to keep his hands off her. He was too damn involved with her: trying to keep her safe; her problem with Brandon's custody. They'd become his problems now. And when the person who was trying to kill her was apprehended, the SOB would have him to deal with.

Kurt and Don finally went to bed, and Ann went into her bedroom to dress for her appointment with Barney Hailey. Since Mike and Cassidy were on watch, they'd accompany her to the restaurant where she was meeting Hailey for lunch.

Much to Ann's relief Barney was already seated and waiting for her. She'd have hated to sit alone with Mike and Dave peering at her from a nearby table.

It was so good to see her ex-boss again. Short in stature, Barney reminded her of an aging Mickey Rooney. His hair was disappearing as fast as his waist was expanding, and he always moved with a hurried step and an unlit cigar perpetually clenched between his teeth.

A legend in the advertising world, he'd won countless awards as a photographer for his unique shots of athletes and models. Fifteen years earlier his wife, Gertie, had persuaded him to come out from behind the camera and start his own agency. Under his keen direction it had become one of the busiest in the industry.

From the time Ann worked for him, they'd always had more than a working relationship. Barney had hired her right from college and taken her under his wing. Due to his tutelage she'd learned what to look for through the lens of a camera, and within a year could recognize a good shot as well, if not better, than many who had years of experience.

Childless, Barney and Gertie had kept a watchful eye over her like protective parents, and Ann would often spend vacation summers at their home in Connecticut.

Barney had been devastated when his beloved Gertie

passed away five years ago, and had thrown himself wholeheartedly into his business to cope with his loss. His accounts had doubled and he even had gone back to taking some of the shots himself.

For Ann, Gertie's death had been like losing her mother all over again. A year later she met Clayton Burroughs. As much as she hated leaving Barney, he had plenty of accomplished photographers; so, suffering with burnout and the need to have a big change in her life, she accepted Clayton's job offer. Barney understood her reason for leaving and remained the Dutch uncle whom she could always phone whenever she felt homesick.

Ann told him the whole story of Clayton's death, the attempts on her life and the legal struggle to gain custody of Brandon. He was clearly concerned for her welfare, but saw her need to get her life back on track. He gave her a shooting schedule for the following morning.

When they finished lunch, upon leaving, he stopped at the table where Mike and Dave were seated. Barney made no attempt to introduce himself or shake hands, but said simply, "Don't you fellows let anything happen to this gal." Then he picked up their lunch check and moved on.

By the time they got back to the apartment after stopping by the office to pick up some camera equipment and film, only four hours remained of their watch. Mike and Cassidy split up the hall shifts to two hours for each of them, and Dave took the first shift.

Ann changed into slacks and a blouse then joined Mike in the kitchen. "Do you want something to drink?" he asked, popping a can of beer.

"Just water," she said.

"So what did your boss have to say about your predicament?" he asked.

''He's concerned for my welfare.'' She grinned. ''I told him I was in good hands.''

Mike took a drink of the beer. ''Your confidence is flattering, Ann, but I'd like to get this over with.''

''Not anymore than I would, Mike.'' She picked up her glass of water and strolled over to the weight room where Kurt and Don were working out. Mike followed her.

''So this is how Kim Barrington maintains her gorgeous figure,'' she said, glancing around her. The room was better equipped than many health clubs. And the squad members were not wasting the opportunity.

Kurt and Don were bare-chested and wearing shorts. They had beautiful, well developed and proportioned bodies, and both had worked up a sweat. Their lithe bodies glistened with perspiration.

Ann couldn't resist the temptation. She got her camera and starting snapping some candid shots of the men.

''Do you intend to use those shots professionally?'' Mike asked.

''Haven't given it any thought. Why do you ask?''

''Just wondering. It could hurt their careers.''

''You mean in the CIA?''

''I'm not talking about *Harper's Bazaar,* Hamilton.''

He walked away.

Ann continued taking shots of them. She even got them to pose together for several more.

Later, after Mike went out for the hall watch, Kurt found some board games in the family room. For the next couple hours Ann and the three men played Trivial Pursuit. At eight o'clock Kurt and Don took over the watch, and Kurt turned on the television set.

With his duty over, Mike put on sweats and started to work out. Dave and Ann played a game of Scrabble.

He beat her mightily in the game, spelling several words she had never heard of before. It wasn't until they were through that he confessed he'd graduated summa cum laude from the University of Virginia.

Ann shook her head in bafflement. This was such an amazing group of men. And there had to be a story behind why a man who graduated with a highest distinction from college would risk his life in a Special Ops squad of the CIA, when he probably could have anchored himself behind a cushy desk with a seven-figure salary in a Fortune 500 company.

As soon as Mike finished his workout, he showered and went to bed. She had failed to get at least one candid shot of Mike working out, and he made it clear he didn't want his picture taken.

Ann smiled to herself. If Mike Bishop thought he was going to get away without her getting a shot of him, he was sadly mistaken. She'd get her picture before it was all over.

Chapter 16

The last few days had passed without incident and Ann had fallen easily back into the routine of life behind the camera lens. In fact, other than her separation from Brandon, things were going so smoothly that she'd relaxed and once again began to doubt she ever had been in danger.

She was explaining this to Mike—unsuccessfully, from the skeptical look on his face, at breakfast before she left for work.

"Trouble is, Mike, people always fixate on old-fashioned superstitions such as...death always comes in threes...or something like the seven-year itch in marriage. Clayton's murder has cast too heavy a shadow on everything that's followed, so when the simplest mishap occurs, it's human nature to stretch the imagination to try and relate it to his death, rather than to mere coincidence."

"Really," he said, and popped a piece of doughnut into his mouth.

He wasn't giving one bit of credibility to what she was

saying. Frustrated, she turned to Cassidy. "Dave, do you understand my point?"

"I understand what you're saying, Ann, but not necessarily your point, because that same theory could be reversed. Because of old-fashioned hang-ups we tend to sluff off mishaps instead of giving them the attention they deserve."

"Dave, don't waste your breath," Mike said. "I've been over this with her, time and time again."

She sighed when he strode away. His temper was becoming shorter with every passing day. They had really begun to get on each other's nerves. They'd been together day and night for more than two weeks—and it sure wasn't a honeymoon.

She had the mental challenge of renewing her career, while he was stuck with a job he didn't even want. He was used to action, and being holed up most of the time in hotel rooms and this apartment was really working on his nerves.

She could relate to that. As much as she'd grown to love the guys in the Dwarf Squad, it was difficult living with four men, and she looked forward to the day when she'd be on her own. When she could walk to the kitchen in her nightgown, or not make sure the bathroom door was locked when she went into shower. Not that any of the men had invaded her privacy. She was just aware they were around.

She had lived alone for too long and enjoyed that solitary life. She knew she would have to adjust to the same problem when Brandon moved in with her, but until then, interacting with people all day was enough for her; she welcomed the sound of silence at the end of the day—no radio, no television and no big men with their heads in the refrigerator every time she looked.

But above all, she needed to distance herself from Mike

Bishop. He dominated her thoughts. It would be good to see how she'd fare without him around. Not for security reasons, but for that time-immemorial battle of the sexes. It was hard to convince herself she could get along without him when her heart started beating every time he was near. She hoped that there was a ring of truth to that old out-of-sight, out-of-mind adage, because she sure was aware of him when he was around.

The drive to work was quiet—that is to say in the interior of their car. The yellow cabs were out in full force. Mike was his usual reticent self, and Dave concentrated on the driving.

To explain their daily presence on the shoot, Barney was passing off Dave Cassidy as his nephew learning the business and Mike as Ann's overly zealous boyfriend. The excuses gave both men the opportunity of remaining near Ann at all times, without appearing to interact with each other.

Ann got special pleasure out of observing the two men during the day. Mike could barely conceal his boredom, but Dave was enjoying the experience immensely. The tall, good-looking agent had caught the eye of more than one of the models, and there was a lot of joshing back and forth between him and the women.

Mike hadn't failed to notice the rapport that had developed the past few days between Cassidy and the models. In passing, Mike said, "Cassidy, keep your mind on what you're here for."

"Same to you, buddy," Cassidy said.

"Your point?"

"Objectivity, Grumpy."

Once back in the chair he'd been occupying, Mike thought of the remark. Cassidy was right. What in hell was wrong with him? He was acting like a love starved schoolboy. He couldn't remain objective when it came to Ann.

He was hot for her. Was always uptight around her. And took out his anger with himself on her.

And he was going frigging out of his mind worrying if something would happen to her!

He leaped to his feet when he recognized the man who approached Ann as she was wrapping up the shoot for the day. How did Ricardo DeVilles know where to find her?

The noose was tightening again.

He hurried over to where DeVilles was fawning over Ann. DeVilles appeared not to be as surprised to see him as Mike had been when the Brazilian showed up. He ignored Mike, mumbled a few words to Ann that Mike could not hear, kissed her hand and then departed.

"How did DeVilles know you were in New York?" Mike questioned as soon as Ann climbed into the car.

"I have no idea, unless he spoke to someone at the State Department," she said.

"That wouldn't explain why he knew where to find you in New York."

"Gee, Agent Bishop, do you suppose he might have called Barney's office and found out?" she asked. "I did leave his number with the British."

"Or it could be you called him and told him where to find you."

"I did not call Ricardo to tell him where I was," Ann declared through gritted teeth. Mike's paranoia was driving her crazy. He didn't trust any of her actions.

She was getting angry with him again, and she didn't want to argue. "I thought of a great theory today while we were using those astrological symbols as a backdrop. Maybe instead of you guys protecting me, I just need an astrologer," she said, shifting to a more frivolous mood. "Maybe my star is on the descendency, Mercury is about to collide with Mars, or some such cosmic cataclysm, and that's why these strange accidents are happening to me." She chuckled at this latest bit of whimsy. "Why not blame it on the stars? That's as good an excuse as any to explain coincidence."

"Or to dismiss what you don't want to accept," Mike said. He turned his head to the window and didn't speak the rest of the ride.

It wasn't until later when she finished dressing for her dinner date with Ricardo that Ann realized she hadn't told Mike she was going out to dinner. She put the finishing touches to her hair and pinned it behind her ears with clips, then stepped back for a final inspection. As she slipped on the black sandals with the three-inch heels she thought of the last time she wore them. Mike had taken her to that delightful Italian restaurant in D.C. He had kissed her that night. Deep in reverie, she stared into the mirror and unconsciously raised her fingers to her lips—she could still feel that kiss.

A light tap on the door jarred her out of her reverie, and Mike came in. As usual he didn't wait to be asked.

"I understand you're not eating…"

He stopped in mid-sentence and stared at her. She was wearing a black dinner gown with spaghetti shoulder straps and a skirt that flowed to her knees. "Where in hell do you think you're going?"

"I'm going to dinner with Ricardo," she said, adjusting an earring.

"No, you're not."

She spun around. "Mike, I am not a member of your squad, so I don't have to take your orders. Whether you like or not, I'm leaving."

"Do you have a death wish, Hamilton?"

"I didn't, until I met you."

"You're not leaving."

"Just watch me."

She picked up her purse and shawl and walked past him. It was a short-lived victory. When she stepped out into the lounge, Cassidy put down his newspaper and stood up.

"Going somewhere, Ann?"

"Out to dinner, Dave." She punched the elevator button. Fortunately the programmed card key wasn't needed to get off the floor, because Mike had it.

"Alone?"

"I'll be joining Ricardo DeVilles."

"Sorry, Ann. I can't let you leave until I clear it with Mike."

He'd no sooner spoken than Mike came out and handed Dave his suit jacket. "Let's not make this too late a night, Hamilton. We all need our sleep." To her further displeasure Kurt and Don joined them.

Ann glared at Mike, the elevator pinged, the doors slid open and she stepped into the elevator.

The four men followed.

Ricardo had reserved a table at the Starlight Room of the Waldorf. His disappointment was evident when Ann joined him accompanied by Mike.

"This is an unexpected pleasure, Mr. Bishop," DeVilles said when Mike sat down at the table.

"Now, you really don't mean that, DeVilles," Mike said.

"I'm sure he doesn't," Ann said, "but at least Ricardo is displaying considerably more graciousness then you deserve, Bishop."

The waiter hurried over and added a plate setting for Mike. DeVilles was too stunned to even notice the three men who'd followed the couple in and were seated at a nearby table.

"Just ignore him, Ricardo. I do," Ann said.

"That would be quite difficult, my dear. Mr....ah, Mike, I applaud the conscientiousness you bring to your job, but would you be offended if I asked you to sit at a different table?''

"Matter of fact, I would, DeVilles," Mike said. "As you've said, I take my responsibilities seriously. And Miss Hamilton is my responsibility. But don't worry, pal, I'll pay for my own dinner."

Mike glanced at the couple on the dance floor. They had remained on the dance floor from the moment the band had started to play. What had gotten into him? He was acting like a child. Throughout the meal he had purposely listened to every word said between them. Invaded their conversation uninvited. But she had driven him to it with her defiance of his orders tonight. God! He'd like to walk away from the whole damn mess. Let what ever might happen happen.

What a crock! He could never walk away. Not now. He was in too deep. And his gut instinct told him that bastard with her was, too. But not for the same reason.

He swung his gaze back to them. They were doing one of those sexy Latin dances that made *Dirty Dancing* look like a Disney movie. Mike clenched his hands into fists. If the creep lowered his hand another inch, he was going to end up toast.

The music ended and the band took a break. Ann and DeVilles came back to the table.

"Curfew time," Mike said. He picked up her shawl and put it around her shoulders.

"I'm not ready to leave, Bishop," Ann declared. "I'm enjoying myself."

"That's unfortunate because it's time to go."

"Feel free to leave, Mr. Bishop. Ann will be safe in my hands," DeVilles said.

"I saw how safe she was in your hands, DeVilles.

Aren't you a little too old to be groping women half your age on the dance floor, pal?''

"How dare you!" Ann said. "Ricardo, I apologize for the man's rudeness.''

"I understand, my dear. And since he has rejected my offer to take you home, I suggest you leave with him before he makes a greater scene.''

"I'm so sorry, Ricardo. Thank you for dinner.''

Mike took her by the elbow and literally forced her to the door. She shrugged out of his grasp when they entered the elevator and didn't say one word in the cab back to the hotel, but he knew she was steaming.

The other three agents arrived in a cab behind them. She ignored them as well in the elevator. Mike unlocked the door and stepped aside for her to enter. Ann walked in, went directly to her room and slammed the door.

Once inside, they all turned and looked at Mike.

"What happened?" Dave said.

Mike shrugged. "She wanted to stay longer." Mike took off his suit jacket and tossed it aside.

"What did you say that made her so angry?" Kurt asked. "She looked like she was ready to blow her top.''

"So maybe I was out of line. I was tired. I needed to get out of there." Mike pulled off his tie and loosened the top buttons of his shirt. "Besides, didn't you see how the guy was practically doing her on the dance floor.''

"Give it up, Mike," Dave said. "They were dancing.''

"And they were good at it, too," Don added.

"It didn't look like that to me." Mike picked up his jacket and tie. "Fraser, aren't you due out in that hall-way?''

The men moved away. Mike was disgusted with himself. He had to get a grip on himself. Get his emotions out of the mix and do the job expected of him.

He tapped on Ann's door and walked in. She was in the

process of undressing and was stripped down to a black bra and half slip. The sight of her rocked him on his heels, and his groin knotted. It took every bit of his reserve to keep his mind on what he'd come in there for.

"Get out of here," she declared, and snatched up a robe from the foot of the bed.

"Ann, I have to talk to you."

"You said more than enough," she said, belting the robe firmly. "I'm not interested in any more you have to say."

"Okay, I was out of line. I admit it."

"That may excuse it in your eyes, Bishop, but not in mine. I can't abide another moment of this chest-pounding machismo of yours. I have no doubt such qualities work in combat, but they or you do not belong in a civilized society. Your conduct tonight proves it. Who do you think you are that you can insult my friends, Bishop? Ricardo DeVilles is a gentleman and you—"

"Ann, I don't trust the man."

"I don't care," she lashed out. "I want you out of my life, Mike. I don't want anymore of your *protection.* Either you leave tomorrow or I do. Now get out of here."

"Don't you think I'd like nothing better?" he said.

"Then do us both a favor and leave me alone."

"I would, if I wasn't dealing with an ostrich with its head stuck in the sand."

"Thank you for that analogy, Bishop, and all because I don't believe there's an assailant behind every tree. That I can't accept your instinct about Ricardo DeVilles, a man I've known and respected for four years. And for the record, Agent Bishop, I intend to go out to lunch with Ricardo tomorrow—*without you.*"

Until then he'd done a credible job of holding on to his temper, but she'd rather defy him than use common sense.

"Why can't you understand why I don't want you to see that man again?"

"Oh, I understand, Mike. You're the one who's confused."

He grabbed her arm. "Your point being?"

She glanced down at his fingers clutched around her flesh then back up at him. For a long moment their gazes locked and held, then her mouth curved into a triumphant smirk when he released her.

"Careful, Mike, you're beginning to act more and more like a jealous husband."

Her jibe hit home. She'd voiced the emotion he'd been denying to himself. He'd begun to think of her as his. The nearness of her, the scent of her, the tension between them—so much deeper than the conflict they were arguing about—and the need to have her became too overwhelming to fight. His control shattered from the hunger of his need.

Pulling her into his arms, he covered the scornful smile on her lips with the hardness of his own mouth. The passion of anger quickly changed into that of desire—a desire that had been churning within him for weeks.

Her long-suppressed ardor ignited to match his, and the kiss deepened until they were forced to break apart. They stared, breathless and startled, into each other's eyes.

The choice was his to make, and he knew it. If there was to be any hope for keeping her alive through this nightmare, he had to get out of that room now.

He reached for the doorknob.

Chapter 17

There was no sign of Mike at breakfast the next morning. When Kurt accompanied her and Cassidy to the shoot instead of Mike, Dave told her Mike had revised the schedules.

So he was avoiding her. It was just as well as far as Ann was concerned. The farther they distanced themselves from each other, the easier it would be for both of them to rationalize their relationship.

Last night's kiss had certainly stirred the smoldering embers between them into flames.

Mike wasn't the only one on her mind that morning, though. She'd thought a great deal about Ricardo last night while she lay in bed. Mike's suspicion about Ricardo having a personal interest in her appeared to be correct. The way he held her while they danced last night was extremely intimate, and went beyond the bounds of platonic friendship.

She'd been very naive about Ricardo. He was Clayton's

close friend, and she had never considered him in a romantic way, any more than she had Clayton.

Fortunately, this was the wrap-up of the shoot so she
was kept busy all morning. It wasn't until Ricardo showed
up to take her to lunch that the problem pressed upon her
again.

"And where is your Mr. Bishop today?" Ricardo asked
when they were seated at the restaurant.

Since he had not met the other squad members, Ricardo
was unaware of Kurt Bolen at a nearby table. Nothing
would be gained by pointing him out to Ricardo, so she
merely shrugged.

"I have no idea, Ricardo. We quarreled last night over
his rudeness to you, and I haven't seen him since."

"Are you saying your watchdog has run away?"

She smiled. "I really don't know. It just feels good not
to have him breathing down my neck when I'm trying to
eat."

"You should have thrown him a bone, my dear."

You have no idea what size bone I threw him when I
returned his kiss, Ricardo. Mike and I will probably be
chewing on last night's kiss for a long time.

Ricardo reached across the table and clasped her hand.
"I'm glad he isn't around, Ann, because there's something
very important I wish to discuss with you."

Ann began to feel uncomfortable. She knew it would be
something of a personal nature, and she had hoped she
wouldn't have to deal with that issue right now. There
were too many other problems on her mind at the moment.

"Will you marry me, Ann?"

Why hadn't she seen this coming? Even though she had
come to suspect Ricardo had deeper feelings for her than
she once believed, she didn't expect this sudden proposal.
She felt distraught. She cared for him and did not want to

hurt him, but she could never marry for any reason except love.

"Ricardo, I care for you so much and I'm flattered by your proposal, but I can't marry you. I'm not in love with you."

"I understand that, Ann, but we're compatible. We have many interests in common. And I can offer you financial security. You wouldn't have to work another day of your life. We could have a very contented existence together."

Contented existence? She wanted more from a marriage than financial security. Contentment to her would be working out the problems and building the marriage together, having children, squabbling with your husband, then making up afterward. She wanted to feel needed—and wanted to need someone in return. And she wanted the Roman candles going off when he kissed her and that sudden surge of love and excitement when he entered a room or simply touched her in passing.

That was contentment—and she would never consider anything less.

"Come back to Brazil with me, Ann," Ricardo pleaded.

"I can't, Ricardo. It would be so tempting to say yes, but it wouldn't be fair to you."

"If it's the danger you're in, I can make certain you will be safe there."

"It's much more than that, Ricardo. There's Brandon to think about and—"

"It's that agent, isn't it?" he suddenly lashed out. "You would reject everything I am offering you for that uncouth, foul-mouthed Bishop. I gave you credit for better taste, Ann."

"Agent Bishop has nothing to do with it. I've explained my reason for refusing your proposal, Ricardo."

"The vulgar pawing of some muscular womanizer is a

poor substitute for what I can offer you. You're making a big mistake, Ann. Greater than you think.''

Ann stood up. ''I think you're overwrought right now, Ricardo. Thank you for lunch. It's not necessary that you see me back to work. Goodbye.''

She just wanted out of there. She couldn't cope with another scene with any man. She wanted them all out of her life—and them to stay out. If a woman rejected *their* wishes, she was at fault. Lord forbid if any one of them could be wrong! Well, this was the last straw. She didn't owe Mike or Ricardo anything. From now on she intended to do exactly what she thought was best for her and Brandon.

Kurt followed her into the cab.

''Can't I have five minutes of freedom from you men?''

''Sorry, Ann. I'm only following orders.''

''I noticed you at the next table. I suppose you heard the conversation.''

''Most of it,'' he said.

''I thought so.'' Ann sighed and looked out the window. *Men!*

After both a physical and mentally exhausting day, Ann had just gotten back to her room when Mike knocked on the door.

''Ann, may I come in?''

That was a new twist on his part—the almighty Mike Bishop asking to come in.

''No,'' she snapped with satisfaction.

He opened the door and came in.

''What part of no don't you understand, Bishop?''

''I don't have time to quibble over words.''

''What do you want?''

''I understand DeVilles threatened you at lunch today.''

"Yeah, right," she said. "He told me I had to pay for my own meal."

"This is serious, Hamilton. Kurt said his closing remarks to you were threatening."

"Will you give it up, Mike? It wasn't a threat to do me bodily harm. He meant that I was giving up a life of milk and honey by turning down his proposal of marriage for… I believe such expressions as *uncouth, foul-mouthed* and *womanizer* entered the conversation."

"To whom was he referring?"

"If I recall, your name did enter the conversation."

"Like it's gonna keep me awake nights. I figure more than ever that I'm right about the schmuck."

"Mike, why would Ricardo ask me to marry him if he intended to kill me?"

"Yeah, like husbands don't murder their wives, Hamilton. It would be a perfect setup. Marry you, get us out of the way and you down there to South America. Then one day you have a fatal accident."

"I may have seen a streak in Ricardo today that I didn't like, but nothing that would make me think he intended to kill me. Let's face it, Bishop, I've seen worse examples in you, and you claim you're trying to keep me alive. Now will you please get out of here so I can change my clothes."

He paused with his hand on the doorknob. "Ah, Ann, I'm sorry about last night. It was my fault. I totally lost it. I think the best solution is to keep my distance."

"Yes, I think you're right, Mike. There's a lot of tension between us, and we're really getting on each other's nerves."

"Let's hope this mess will be over soon." He opened the door and departed.

She suddenly felt overwhelmed with loneliness.

*   *   *

True to his word, Mike avoided her the rest of the evening.

She missed him already. She was such a vacillating wimp. No matter how mad she might get, she'd never been able to stay angry with anyone. And despite all she'd told herself about distancing herself from Mike, she was miserable, and regretted the horrible, nasty things she'd said to him. He'd had the decency to apologize, why hadn't she done the same when she had the chance?

Ann went to bed that night with a troubled mind. Stay the course, Ann. You're doing the right thing.

She would have to live with it, and it shouldn't hurt as much after a few more days.

The next day they were doing a shoot on an old vessel in the harbor for a capri pants advertisement that tied in to a popular pirate movie. It helped to raise Ann's spirits somewhat because she would be working with Amy Heather, one of her favorite models.

The girl's career had been on the ascent when Ann had left the agency, and in the past four years Amy had become one of Barney's top models. In the time they had worked together, Amy had looked upon Ann as a mentor. Always punctual, she had a warm, sweet personality, and was even-tempered. Whatever the hours or length of the shoot, Amy would do it without complaint.

Things started to go wrong from the start. One of the spotlights blew, and they were delayed waiting for a replacement bulb. They had no sooner resumed shooting than, while waiting for a difficult backdrop, Amy spilled a cup of coffee over herself and had to have a change of wardrobe.

They were near wrapping up the shoot when Mother Nature got into the act and it started to rain. It was more like a light sprinkle, so rather than cancel the shoot and finish it off the next day, they decided to wait out the rain.

The only good thing Ann found thus far about the day was that Ricardo did not show up. She half expected he would. Not that she wanted him to. Her initial anger with him had passed, but she was in no mood to deal with their problem. Since she had never asked where he was staying in New York, she would call him at his home in Rio de Janeiro in a couple days.

The bad thing was that there still was no sign of Mike. She had thought he would show up on the set, but Kurt and Dave had accompanied her.

"Hope this rain stops soon," Amy said, peering out the door of the trailer in which they had taken refuge.

"I just need a couple more shots," Ann said. "Do you mind working a little longer today?"

"No, it will just be a relief to get rid of this darn wig," Amy said. She took off the black wig she was wearing and shook out her blond hair. "Oh, does that feel good."

"Looks good on you, honey," Ann said.

"Yes, but these wigs are so warm. It's like wearing a wool cap in this heat. Whose idea was it for me to wear the darn thing?"

"No matter what you wear, Amy, you always look like the all-American girl. Barney thought a black wig would make you appear more swashbuckling. He even wants me to take a few extra shots of you with a bandanna—Gucci, of course—wrapped around your head and a gold loop in your ear."

"What, no parrot?" Amy exclaimed.

It cracked them both up and they broke into laughter.

By the time it stopped sprinkling the sun had set. Dave and Kurt helped Ann set up the lights and they were finally ready to shoot the final shots on the ship.

"Thank goodness," Amy said, waiting for the shot.

"Get that wig on, Amy," Ann said.

"Oh, I forgot and left it in the trailer," she said.

"I'll get it. Barney wants those bandanna shots, too. Wait here, honey, I'll be right back."

Dave and Kurt were standing together in front of the trailer when she hurried up. "Ready to go?" Dave asked.

"Just a couple more shots and we're through," Ann said. She gathered up the wig, bandanna and the gold ear loop. "I'd appreciate your help, though, breaking down those spots later."

"Sure thing," Kurt said. "Ann, has Amy got a steady?"

"Not really. Why?"

"The guy's been drooling over her all day," Dave said.

"I noticed you and Amy were rather chummy. You want me to fix you up?" she asked.

"Just let me know the lay of the land," Kurt said. "I'll do my own asking."

"Will Mike let you out for the night?" she teased.

He winked at her. "I'm off duty at eight."

She started back when the force of a loud explosion threw her to the ground. Stunned, she raised her head. The fiery remains of the ship lit up the dock.

Chapter 18

Dave and Kurt had also been thrown to the ground from the shock of the explosion. "Are you okay?" Dave asked as they got up and helped her to her feet. Ann nodded.

"Where's Amy?" Kurt asked.

Still slightly dazed, Ann stared in horror at the remains of the blazing ship. "On the ship," she said in despair.

Struck by the full impact of her words, in near hysteria she cried out, "She was on the ship," just as Mike and Don Fraser raced up to them.

"Anybody hurt here?" Mike asked.

Ann was too dazed to wonder where he came from, or why he was there. Her eyes were wide and liquid with mounting hysteria. "Mike, Amy's on the ship."

"I'll cover her," Mike said, putting his arms around her. He nodded toward the ship. "Check it out." The three agents sped away.

The heat of the blaze was tremendous and drove back the men. Patches of burning oil and debris floated on the water as they scanned it.

"There. Over there," Dave said, pointing to an object. "It looks like a body."

"It is," Kurt said.

They shoved their weapons and wallets into Don's hands and the two men dove into the water.

Attracted by the explosion and blaze, a crowd had begun to gather by the time they'd recovered Amy's body. Don put his head to her chest.

"She's got a heartbeat."

Fiery cinders sparked the air and smoke stung the eyes and nostrils. The night was rent with the sound of sirens as emergency vehicles raced up and screeched to a halt.

A crew of paramedics shoved the agents aside and took over with Amy. She had not sustained any burns, and the fact that she'd been on the opposite end of the ship had kept her from going up with the ship when it exploded. However, it was too soon to determine if it'd been enough to save her life. The force of the explosion had blown her off the ship, and the medics had no way of determining the severity of internal injury she had sustained. They put her on a gurney and rushed the unconscious model away to the hospital.

Mike had made Ann go inside the trailer and sit down while she related to the police what had preceded the explosion. Then they thanked her and left her alone.

Tears welled in her eyes as she looked at the articles still clutched in her hand—a wig, bandanna and an earring. With loving strokes she smoothed out the strands of the black wig. The image of the long, black curls dangling to Amy's shoulders brought a tender smile to Ann.

Mike stuck his head in the door. "We can leave now, Ann."

Without conscious awareness she stuffed the articles into her purse, and then she stepped outside.

It was a drastic change from the earlier holocaust. The

crowd had dispersed and now only a single squad car remained and a few firemen hosed down the charred remains of the ship.

Mike had called Barney to inform him what happened, and he was already at the hospital when they arrived.

"How is she?" Ann asked as soon as they joined him.

"Don't know too much," Barney said. "She's regained consciousness and they took a lot of MRI's and other tests. The doc said they're pretty certain there's no brain damage, and she can move her arms and legs, which is a good sign that there's no spinal damage, either. But he said the shock from the blast and being blown into the water could very likely have caused internal damage. It'll take a couple days before they complete all their tests and know the results."

"May I see her?" Ann asked.

"Doc says for just a few minutes. I've been waiting until you arrived. They've given her something to kill the pain and help her to sleep, so we better go in now."

Mike and the rest of the squad waited outside Amy's room while Ann and Barney went inside. When they came out, Ann had some of the color back in her face and her spirits had perked up a little after talking to Amy.

"How is she doing?" Kurt asked.

"She's pretty doped up, but she still smiled. She said she hoped we got the license number of the truck that hit her."

Barney pulled Mike aside. "Do the police know what caused the explosion?"

"They think the hot lights all day on that old, decayed wood caused a spontaneous combustion, and the fire then crept to the fuel tank."

"That makes sense," Barney said.

"I'm not buying it," Mike replied.

"Why not?"

"None of us saw or smelled a fire until the ship exploded. And it rained most of the afternoon. How could the wood have been *that* dry?"

"So you're thinking someone deliberately started the fire," Barney said.

"Look, pal, there's a damn good reason why we've been trying to protect Ann. And I think we better get her out of here. She still looks pretty peaked."

Barney went over to Ann and told her not to worry about coming to work tomorrow. Then he hugged her and told her to try to get a good night's sleep.

Once back at the apartment, Ann went directly to her room. Shortly after, Dave brought her a sandwich and a cup of tea.

"I'll take the tea, but I don't want the sandwich. I'm not hungry. And you can tell your boss I'm fine, Dave, so you guys don't have to treat me like I'm an invalid."

"I'll deliver your message."

"And, Dave, thanks. I'm glad you men were there tonight. I don't think I'd have gotten through it without you."

"Sure you would. You've got a lot of grit, Miss Ann Hamilton." He picked up the sandwich plate. "And don't forget to drink that tea." He winked at her and grinned. "We spiked it."

Smiling, she picked up the cup and took a sip of the tea. She almost choked. He hadn't exaggerated. There was enough brandy in it to curl her hair. She drank the whole cup.

Soon the brandy kicked in and Ann began to relax. She took a shower and washed her hair to get the smell of smoke out of it.

Then she put on pajamas and climbed into bed. Thanks to the effects of the brandy, she slept soundly throughout the night.

* * *

The next morning when she left her room, all four of the men were seated around the table, which was unusual; Mike had always insisted one man be stationed in the lounge when she was there.

She paused before entering the kitchen when she heard Mike say, "Okay, let's brainstorm. We've all worked with explosives and know that a timer wouldn't have been used to detonate the charge."

"So if it wasn't an accident, a remote was used," Dave said.

"But it doesn't make sense," Don said. "If Ann was the intended victim, he'd have to be close enough to know that she was on the ship. So why would he blow it when she wasn't?"

"He thought she was," Kurt said.

"Why? Amy Heather has dark hair and Ann is a blonde," Mike questioned.

"Amy is a blonde, too, Mike. That was a wig she was wearing." Kurt suddenly snapped his fingers. "Come to think of it—"

"She *wasn't* wearing the wig at the time of the explosion," Dave interjected, finishing the sentence. "That's why Ann came back to the trailer to get it."

"And so whoever it was mistook Amy for Ann and blew the ship," Mike said. "Mistaken identity!"

"I wouldn't doubt that's what happened to that lawyer Ann's been trying to find, too," Dave said.

"Charles Breton?"

Dave nodded. "He and his yacht are probably at the bottom of the ocean."

"Yeah, but don't you think someone would have spotted some wreckage by now?" Don asked.

Dave snorted. "Yeah, if they knew where to start looking."

"Dave's right, Don," Kurt said. "There's a lot of ocean out there and no one knows where or when it happened."

"There's another possibility we aren't considering," Mike said. "Maybe this Breton is behind Burroughs's death and the attempts on Ann's life."

"Motive being?" Kurt asked.

Mike shrugged. "How the hell would I know? I understand Burroughs was loaded. If Breton handled the guy's estate, could be he swindled him and Burroughs discovered it."

"Too simple," Dave said. "I don't think the Agency would get involved if they didn't think it was all linked to the sabotage of that satellite."

"I'm not so sure of that," Kurt said. "The Agency deals in intrigue, so they pin that label on everything and end up complicating the issue."

"You've got that right," Mike said.

Ann heard all she wanted to. Disturbed by all she'd overheard, she went back to her room. If they were right about Charles Breton, it would mean there'd be an indefinite delay in settling the custody of Brandon.

Against Mike's orders, she picked up the telephone and put in a call to England. The sound of Brandon's voice was music to her ears after the chaos and near tragedy of the previous evening.

"I don't want to stay here anymore, Ann," Brandon said. He started to cry. "Why can't I stay with you?"

"You can soon, darling."

"Please come and get me. I miss you and Grandfather. Please, Ann?"

"Darling, I'm doing whatever I can to arrange for us to be together. It's taking longer than I thought."

"Then why don't you come back here? If you love me, you'd come back to be with me. Please, Ann. Please come back."

"I will, darling."

"Pro-promise," he sobbed.

"I promise, sweetheart. I'll figure out a way I can get you."

She finally succeeded in getting him to stop crying, but by the time she hung up, she was on the verge of tears. The whole situation was too heartwrenching.

Ann opened her purse to get a tissue to wipe her eyes. She paused in surprise and pulled out the wig and stared blankly at it. When had she put these items in her purse?

She fingered the wig. Mistaken identity. That's what Mike had said.

Suddenly she thought of a simple solution to the problem about Brandon. Just what the men were discussing. Sometimes by overlooking the obvious, the issue becomes too complicated. Valuable time had been wasted by doing just that.

The time had come to take matters into her own hands. Reaching for the telephone again, she dialed information.

Five minutes later Ann hung up. She calmly calculated her next move. She had put the ball in motion, now all she had to do was get out of the apartment undetected. And if her luck held, there would never be a better time than now.

Grabbing her purse, she checked the contents to make sure she had everything she needed, then she opened the bedroom door and peeked out. The drone of the men's voices still sounded from the kitchen—the war room was still plotting their strategy.

Ann cautiously crossed to the door and stepped out into the lounge. Her luck hadn't run out. General Bishop had called in the troops, and there was no one there on duty.

She pushed the elevator button and held her breath as she listened to the whir of the ascending elevator. Within seconds the doors opened.

On the way down she pulled the black wig out of her purse and put it on. If anyone *was* watching the building, he'd be looking for a blonde.

The doorman was assisting a woman out of a cab when she got outside. Ann walked away hurriedly before he could even make eye contact with her and was instantly swallowed up by the teeming pedestrians.

A block farther she flagged down a cab, and exactly seventy minutes later she settled back in the seat of a plane bound for Kourou.

It had all been so simple—so uncomplicated.

Chapter 19

It was late when the taxi pulled up in front of her condo in Kourou. Ann told the driver to wait. It would take just a few minutes to get her copy of the codicil out of the safe, and then she would get back to the airport. That way she wouldn't be tempted to hang around and start packing up her belongings.

The sooner she got out of there and back to New York, the less angry Mike might be. As much as she hated breaking her promise to him, she had Brandon's interests to consider, too.

Ann retrieved the spare key from the false bottom of her mailbox and unlocked the door. As soon as she turned on the light, she gasped with shock. The place had been ransacked: drawers and cupboards were left open and cushions pulled off chairs and sofas.

Her bedroom was in just as bad condition. Shoeboxes had been yanked off closet shelves and dumped on the floor, as well as the desk and dresser drawers. It was almost as bad as what those abductors had done to the bedroom at the mountain villa.

She wanted to cry, but what would that solve? The object was to stay the course—get the codicil out of the safe and go directly back to the airport. The mess could be cleaned up later when she returned to pack up.

Whoever had searched the house must have done it so hastily that the culprit failed to discover the wall safe hidden behind one of the pictures. He probably didn't expect her to have a safe, and she wouldn't have had one, either, if the previous owner hadn't had it installed.

Ann grabbed the codicil, kissed the document and stuffed it into her purse. Then she swung the strap over her shoulder and across her breast like a bandolier of ammunition. Nothing or no one was going to separate her from that purse. On the spur of the moment she grabbed a suitcase and quickly threw some pieces of lingerie, a couple of pairs of shoes, blouses and slacks into it. Seeing her expensive camera equipment lying on the floor, on impulse she picked up her favorite camera and shoved some rolls of film into the suitcase as well. And remembering the wig, she pulled it off, relieved to get the hot thing off her head.

After a final quick look around, Ann grabbed the suitcase, turned off the light and locked the door on her way out.

She hurried down the walk and came to an abrupt halt. The taxi was gone. Even if the driver hadn't heard her tell him to wait, why would he leave without being paid? This latest setback was frustrating. She was on a tight schedule to get back to the airport to catch the return flight to the United States.

Ann hurried back into the house to telephone for a taxi, only to discover the telephone was dead. Slamming it down, she tried again, but there was no dial tone. Why? She hadn't ordered it disconnected.

What now? This was a residential neighborhood; there'd be no cruising cabs to hail. All she could do was try to wake one of her neighbors. So much for slipping in and out unobserved.

She was about to go outside to ring the doorbell of the neighbor when the lights went out. Ann gasped with fright. Too late she realized that none of this was coincidence. Someone was out there stalking her. Would it do any good to scream? Her neighbor was a seventy-five-year-old retired schoolteacher with defective hearing. The condos had cement walls between them to muffle sound and deter fire. If the woman was asleep it was unlikely she'd hear her screams.

Why hadn't she listened to Mike? Heeded his warnings? As if she could out think or outsmart people trained in covert action. Think, Ann. Don't panic. She had no weapon, but she was a fast runner. If she got enough of a head start, she might be able to outrun him. Of course if he had a weapon, she'd be an easy target. That was the chance she had to take. It was better than standing there like a sacrificial lamb waiting for the slaughter.

Ann's heartbeat was deafening in her ears as she listened for the slightest sound. She saw, rather than heard, two shadowy outlines cross the living room window outside. That meant there were at least two of them and they were headed for the front door.

Crouching down, she moved to the kitchen. After carefully slipping the chain off the back door, she unlocked the dead bolt and eased the door open.

The yard looked deserted. If she made it undetected to the copse of trees about fifteen yards away, there was a good chance they might think she was still hiding in the house.

As soon as she heard the front door open, she eased the kitchen door closed and took off at a run. She heard them shout, the door slam and the sound of footsteps in pursuit.

She made it into the trees when suddenly a hand clamped over her mouth and she was literally swung off her feet and pulled against a hard body.

''Quiet and don't make a sound.''

Awake or in her dreams, she would recognize Mike's voice anywhere. She wanted to cry with joy, collapse in his arms and throw her arms around his neck. Everything would be all right. Mike was here. How never entered her thoughts.

He released her and motioned her to crouch down. She didn't hesitate but did as told. When he drew a wicked-looking knife out of his boot, reality set in again and she started to tremble.

Peering through the darkness, she saw the two figures enter the trees and split up. One of them moved closer to where she was crouching. Ann turned her head to look at Mike and discovered he was gone. Where was he?

The man was practically on top of her now. In a few seconds he'd have to be blind not to see her. She was seized with panic and wanted to jump up and run.

Suddenly Mike appeared from behind him and grabbed the man around the neck. She clamped a hand over her mouth to keep from screaming when Mike gave the man's head a quick jerk and he fell to the ground.

Gunshots shattered the night's stillness. Mike dove to the ground as bullets sprayed the area, splintering the tree limb above his head. Then suddenly the firing ceased as quickly as it had begun.

Ann was horrified. Was Mike hurt? He'd ordered her not to move, but she couldn't sit still if he was wounded or possibly even...

Without any thought of her own welfare she crawled

over to where she had seen him fall. There was no sign of him. She looked around in desperation and knew she was in the right spot because a shattered tree limb hung limply from the tree.

When she saw a body on the ground, she choked on her sobs and crawled over to it. With a mixture of horror and relief she stared down at the lifeless face of the dead man. It wasn't Mike, but the face was familiar. Then she had a total recall when she realized where she had seen it before. He was the man who had attacked her when she was jogging in D.C.

Ann stared transfixed into the darkness until a figure approached. A pair of boots came into view, and she followed them upward to the figure looming above her.

With a cry of joy she jumped to her feet and threw herself into Mike's arms. His arms tightened around her and he held her trembling body against the steely strength of his own.

"It's okay, baby," he whispered.

"Are you hurt?" she asked when she was finally able to speak.

"No." He gave a short, quick whistle, and seconds later Dave Cassidy stepped out of the shadows. The men exchanged a glance and Cassidy nodded.

She didn't have to ask about the other gunman. Their body language said it all. She felt the nausea begin to churn in her stomach.

"Hi, Ann," Dave said simply.

"Mike, this man is the one who attacked me in Washington."

"That doesn't surprise me. Remember the guy I pointed out to you in the restaurant in London?"

"The man reading the newspaper."

Mike nodded. "He won't be reading any more headlines."

"You mean they were together."

"Yeah. Let's get out of here."

His statement jolted her back to the here and now. "Not until I lock up my house. I don't want to leave it open. I do have valuables in there."

"Then let's get it over with. Those shots must have wakened some of the neighbors."

There was enough moonlight coming through the windows and open door for Mike and Dave to see the mess inside the house. Dave let out a long whistle as he looked around at it. "They really trashed the place."

"It's difficult to say at this point, but I didn't notice anything in particular missing. I doubt whoever did it was a thief."

Mike gave her one of his condescending looks. "No, Ann, it wasn't a thief."

"Well I wish I knew what they're looking for."

"Looks pretty amateurish to me," Dave said. "A professional wouldn't have made a mess like this. And vandals would have smashed some of your knickknacks or even sprayed the walls. Unless, of course—"

"Unless what?" she asked.

"Unless whoever did it wanted to make it appear like they were amateurs," Mike said. "Lock up and let's get out of here."

"What in hell is that?" he asked when she picked up the suitcase she'd previously packed.

"Just a couple of things I packed to take back with me."

He grabbed it from her. "Are you able to run?" he asked when the sound of approaching sirens sounded in the distance.

"Just try and keep up with me," she challenged with more spirit than she felt.

"Then let's get going or we'll get stuck answering a lot of questions."

As soon as she locked up the front and rear doors, Dave grabbed her suitcase, Mike her hand, and they raced back into the trees to a parked car a block away.

"How did you know where to find me?" she asked as the car sped away.

Mike gave her a disgruntled look. Now that the danger was past, he was holding his temper in check, but she knew she was in for a real tongue lashing when they were safely out of there.

"I figure you'd head for here or England, so I checked the flight lists."

"Yes, but how did you get here so fast?"

"I know an ex-SEAL who operates a flight school. He owed me a big favor and I called in the tab."

"You mean the CIA didn't pull strings. That's a switch."

"I didn't want to involve them. But don't knock the Agency, Hamilton. You'd have been toast a long time ago if it weren't for them." The anger he was trying to suppress was beginning to slip past his control.

A disturbing thought suddenly crossed her mind. "Mike, what if those were policemen back there?"

"Policemen would have rung your bell and not cut the damn phone and electric lines," Mike shouted in a burst of anger.

He was too angry to listen to her, so she wisely let him have the last word and remained silent for the remainder of the trip.

Once again she found herself being hustled onto a waiting plane at an abandoned airstrip. Mike introduced her to his friend Jack, and as soon as they took off Mike and Dave proceeded to sleep the rest of the flight back to the United States.

Ann also dozed off and woke up when they landed in Florida. Mike shook hands with Jack, said goodbye and thanked him for his help. Then they climbed into a gray BMW and drove off.

When it appeared Mike had no intention of telling her where they were headed, curiosity got the better of Ann and she finally came right out and asked.

"Where you'll be safe," he murmured in his succinct fashion. He had this infuriating ability of never answering a question totally.

"I felt safe in New York," she said.

"Before or after the ship blew up in the harbor?"

"You mean you think that was deliberate, too?"

"Damn straight. Hamilton, you attract disasters. I felt safer on missions in the Middle East than baby-sitting you."

"I never asked you to." The armistice was over.

She folded her arms and stared out the window. What was the sense in arguing with the bullhead?

They stopped three hours later to refill the gas tank, eat and switch drivers. Dave climbed into the back seat and immediately fell asleep.

"It's amazing how you guys can sleep on cue," she said.

"Part of the job. We have to grab the opportunity when we can," he said. "We've got a long drive ahead of us. If you want to climb into the back seat and lie down, Dave can shift up front."

Ann couldn't believe her eyes when he suddenly grinned. It was an engaging break from the frown he'd been wearing. She couldn't help smiling. "What's so funny?"

"Reminded me of my youth," he said. "It's been a long time since I suggested a girl climb into the back seat."

It was clear what he meant. "I might have guessed you were that juvenile, Bishop," she said in disgust.

"You're the most uptight female I've ever met. You

mean that even just once little Miss Prim-and-Proper Hamilton didn't…ah…assume the missionary position in the back seat of a car?"

"Of course I didn't! Is your mind ever on anything but sex, Bishop?"

"Are you talking past sex or future?"

"Present?" she said.

"It's presently on sex," he said, "thinking about future sex when it'll be payback time, sweetheart, and I'll extract my pound of flesh." He grinned again. "Little humor there."

"Little is right. I hope you aren't referring to me. I thought I made myself very clear on that subject, so let's move on to a different one, please."

"You brought it up."

She leaned forward and turned on the radio. To her dismay an orchestra was playing "Someone To Watch Over Me." It was one of her favorite songs, and under any other circumstances she would have leaned back and enjoyed the music. Flustered, she started to turn the dial.

"Leave it on," he said.

"I didn't think a romantic ballad was your kind of music," she said quickly to cover up her agitation.

"Romantic ballad? I thought this was your theme song, Hamilton."

"Very funny, Mike. Since we've got a long ride together, why don't you drop the sarcasm and try to be pleasant."

"Okay, I agree. Since you've caught me at a weak moment, I won't think of it as *your* song. From now on, it'll be *our* song."

Oh, he was so exasperating, but she had to grin. It was hard to stay angry with a man who repeatedly had saved her life. She was so indebted to him, yet they antagonized each other at every turn. And underneath it all was the physical attraction they felt. He was candid about it, but it was getting harder and harder for her to keep denying it knowing he didn't believe her for a second. Was he serious about pursuing her when this was over?

She leaned back and listened to the mellow strains of the music. There was an undeniable excitement in listening to a romantic ballad while riding through the night sitting next to Mike Bishop in the intimacy of the front seat of a car. The sensual essence of him was very provocative.

Lord help me if he ever does try to talk me into that back seat.

"Where are we going, Mike?" she asked, hoping he'd tell her this time.

"Wisconsin."

"We're driving all the way to Wisconsin...in a borrowed car. How do you expect to get this car back to Jack?"

"It's my car. He keeps it in his garage for when I come down to visit him."

"I thought you said you own a place in Wisconsin."

"I do. But I wouldn't keep my Beamer there. I use a pickup."

"So I gather you come to Florida often."

"Yeah, I like the ocean."

"I do, too," she murmured. She closed her eyes and relaxed.

Ann dozed on and off during the night. She would wake up when they made a pit stop to fuel up or change drivers, then fall back to sleep once they were underway again.

As they ate breakfast in Nashville, she offered to drive.

"I thought about it, but you don't have a driver's license with you. If we're stopped for any reason, it would call attention to us."

She hadn't thought of that. Her driver's license was in

her purse that was left back at Clayton's villa when they rescued her and Brandon. Would she ever get her life restored to the proper order?

The miles and hours sped past rapidly. They ate lunch in Indianapolis and supper in Milwaukee. The sun had set by the time Mike drove up to a small cottage bordering on the edge of the Nicolet Forest in Northern Wisconsin.

"Get comfortable, Ann," he said, putting down her suitcase in the only bedroom. "It's no swanky New York apartment, but you blew that."

He opened several windows to get some fresh air flowing through the closed up cabin, turned on the gas and lit the hot water tank. Then he and Dave returned to the car, conversed for several minutes and Dave drove away. Mike came back inside and without any further conversation flopped down on the bed and fell asleep immediately.

Chapter 20

For a long moment Ann stood at the foot of the bed and studied the sleeping figure. Mike was a difficult man to understand. What did he do for enjoyment? Surely he didn't enjoy the brutality of the job he'd chosen. From what he had told her about his father being in the CIA, it hadn't sounded as if Mike had joined by choice but because it was expected of him.

She had thought hard about him on the plane trip to Kourou. The volatility of their last argument weighed heavily on her mind. At times his attitudes were so offensive, they were intolerable. But no matter how hostile he appeared to be at times, she'd been around him long enough to see that it was just a facade. He was a man driven by extreme loyalties. Doing what was expected of him. He would never betray those he loved or those who trusted him or depended on him.

That's why he took his role as squad leader so seriously. He held himself responsible for the life of every man on that team.

She'd witnessed the guilt he tried to conceal the night he'd told her of Tony Sardino's death. She hadn't understood it then. Had even misread his apathetic attitude that led her to believe he thought the man had been careless to let it happen. But now that she understood Mike Bishop she knew, for whatever reason, that he believed he was responsible for Tony Sardino's death.

You're a complicated man, Mike Bishop. Arrogant, dogmatic, bullheaded, and the most exasperating man I've ever known. But the Stockholm Syndrome has claimed another captive because I'm afraid I've falling in love with you. And, try as I might, I can't stop myself.

She pulled off his shoes, and as she set them aside she noticed his cell phone on the bed table. Ann picked it up and went into the other room and dialed Barney. She had some explaining to do to him.

To her relief, her boss was more concerned than angry. With Amy Heather injured, Barney wouldn't consider bringing in a new model, and told her he had permanently canceled the shoot.

"But where are you, Annie?"

"I can't tell you, Barney, but I'm in good hands so don't worry."

"How long will you be gone?"

"I honestly don't know." Mike and the squad would be returning to duty soon, so she said, "I don't think it will be more than a couple of weeks. The good news, Barney, is that I've got the codicil, which should clear up the obstacle concerning Brandon's guardianship. Then I can get my life back on track." If someone doesn't kill me first. Somehow that thought wasn't as amusing as she'd tried to make it. After promising to call him again in a couple of days, she said goodbye and hung up.

As long as Mike was sleeping, she decided it would be a good time to take a shower. Returning to the bedroom, she moved quietly to her suitcase. Laying aside her camera, she began to pull out clean clothes. An intriguing idea entered her mind and she glanced at the sleeping figure on the bed. Why not?

Ann picked up the camera and quickly loaded it, then she returned to the bed and snapped several pictures of Mike from different angles. Pleased with herself, she returned the camera to her suitcase, gathered up the clean clothing and went into the bathroom and locked the door.

The shower and shampoo made her feel like a new woman. To her surprise Mike wasn't on the bed when she came out of the bathroom. Dave Cassidy had returned, and the two men were seated at the kitchen table eating.

"Waterman called me and I told him where you are," Cassidy said. He glanced up and saw her in the doorway. "Hi, Ann."

She crossed the room and sat down with them. "Good thing you got out of that shower," Mike said. "I was about to pound on the door. Your sandwich is getting cold."

She removed the wrapping from around the hamburger heaped with onions, pickles and mushrooms, and catsup spilling over the edges of the bun. It was a towering mound of calories and cholesterol.

"Hope you like mushrooms, Ann," Dave said.

"Yes, it's fine, Dave. Thank you."

"I can tell she's not happy, Dave," Mike said.

"You're so wrong, Bishop," Ann denied. To prove her point she stretched her jaw as wide open as she could and sank her teeth into the sandwich.

"Careful or you'll choke on it," Mike said. "Our job is to keep you alive."

Her mouth was too full to offer a retort.

"Waterman wants you to call him as soon as possible," Dave said, resuming his conversation with Mike. "He asked if the squad was with you, and I told him we weren't. It was the truth at the moment. Then he asked if I knew where Ann is, and I said I didn't know. He's pissed, Mike. You better call him and fill him in. When he finds out I lied to him, he'll probably kick both our asses out of the Agency.''

"Yeah, you're right. I'll call him when I go into town.''

Ann swallowed hard to get the food down her throat. "Your cell phone works fine. I used it to call Barney. Hope you don't mind.''

"You called New York!''

There certainly had to be a worse crime in the world, but from his outburst and the look he and Dave exchanged she was hard-pressed to guess what it might be.

"I'll pay for the call, Mike, if that's what's bothering you.''

"Are you always totally clueless, lady?''

She felt like cowering under his glowering look of anger, and glanced helplessly at Dave. He shifted his gaze downward.

"Why do you think we drove all the way here from Florida instead of taking a flight?'' Mike asked.

"I assumed because Jack couldn't fly us here.''

"Tell her, Dave.'' He turned away in disgust.

"Ann, Jack would have had to file a flight schedule,'' Dave said. "And a commercial liner has a passenger manifest—''

"And,'' Mike interrupted, "whoever is after you is damn clever. Since you never used your return flight ticket, he'll naturally start checking private carriers. Jack had gone in and out of Kourou under the radar, so there's no record of his flight. He'd never get away with it in daylight here in the States. So it would force our clever friend to check out commercial and private flights to other countries and, when you don't turn up on any, we were hoping he'd figure that you're hiding in Kourou or somewhere in

French Guiana since we deliberately avoided any electronic trail such as credit cards or bank withdrawals.''

"Why is that changed now?" she asked.

"Because you used my cell phone to call your boss. Whoever's behind this probably knows my number, and cell phone numbers are easy to check out. Up until now no one had any way of knowing if I was with you. When the mystery man finds out the call went to Hailey from right here in the States, he'll figure we're together and start checking me out. It won't take him too long to find out what he's looking for. In a couple days somebody will be sniffing around up here." He glanced at Cassidy. "You thinking what I am?"

Cassidy nodded. "Yeah, I'll get moving right away." Mike followed Dave out to the car.

Ann felt nauseated and dizzy. Her stomach was spinning as fast as her head. She had ruined everything. All the effort and planning that had gone into the operation was now for naught. Thanks to her it would only buy them a few days. She sat down at the table in despair, propped up her elbows and cradled her head in her hands.

When Mike came back in, she lifted her head. "I'm sorry, Mike."

"Sorry doesn't cut it."

"I know, Mike, but if you'd told me your plans, this wouldn't have happened."

"So now it's my fault. Maybe if you'd listen to me, it's for damn sure it wouldn't have happened. Dammit, Ann, you promised you'd obey my orders and the first chance you got, you broke your word and ran off to Kourou. I've had it with you. I'll be glad when you're out of my hair and somebody else has the headache."

His words stung her pride as much as her heart. Aside from Brandon, Mike had become the most important person in her life—and all she was to him was a headache.

"I'm sorry, Mike, but with each of my conversations with Brandon he'd grown more miserable. I couldn't wait any longer for anyone to try and locate Charles Breton. He must have met the same fate as Clayton. You know that as well as I do. In the meantime, Brandon's the one who's suffering."

"So the kid's unhappy right now. He'll get over it."

"Mike, he's only six years old. He doesn't understand any of what's happening."

"And you're twenty-eight, and apparently you don't, either. How do I get through to you that he'd be suffering a lot more if Dave and I would have arrived in Kourou a few minutes later than we did? Whoever's behind this has got a lot of connections, Ann. One of these times he's going to get lucky. If you don't have sense enough to grasp that and take the necessary precautions then we're wasting our time trying to keep you alive."

"If so, then it would be my fault. Certainly not yours."

He lashed out with bridled fury. "It will be mine if it happens on my watch!"

"That's the real issue here, isn't it, Mike? You mustn't besmirch that gung-ho reputation of yours. Mike Bishop the consummate warrior. God-and-Country Bishop. Americans can sleep peacefully at night knowing Mike Bishop and his Dwarf Squad are watching over them."

His lips were thinned in anger and his hostile glare drilled into her. "What do you want from me, Ann? All I'm doing is trying to keep you alive."

"And you don't try to see beyond the mission. You don't see the desperation in the woman or the heartache in the little boy you're dealing with. People don't have faces or feelings to you. Only names. And even then you prefer to strip them of that dignity by giving them code names: Snow White, Boy Blue, Prince Charming. That makes it even easier for you to remain emotionally uninvolved, doesn't it?''

"Who told you those names?"

"You must think I'm a total idiot! I've overheard you and the squad talking, *Grumpy*,'' she said, deliberately using his code name. "It's not difficult to put the pieces together. Dave is Doc. Kurt is Sneezy, Don is Dopey. Williams is Happy and Bledsoe is Sleepy. Baker is obviously Prince Charming because while were talking to Mr. Waterman you referred to Prince Charming as returning to duty the same time as your squad.''

Smile lines crept from the corners of his eyes as anger filtered into amusement in another of his sudden mood changes. "Not so, Snow White. Williams is Sleepy and Bledsoe is Happy.''

"Big deal! What sense is there to those stupid names? If I can figure them out anyone can.''

"Normally we deal with people who don't have as close a relationship with the squad as you do. That's why a code name is used to designate an individual without revealing the person's real identity.''

"More of the juvenile-boy games you men have to play. It ranks right up there with making out in the back seat of automobiles.''

"Is your mind always on sex, Hamilton?"

He was laughing at her! Her anger rose off the Richter scale. Somehow their roles had reversed. Her intention to thwart his irritation with reasoning had resulted, instead, in raising her ire and amusing him. He did this to her all the time.

She took a deep breath, and then said calmly. "Mike, my concern for Brandon is the only reason I'd *ever* break my word to you. And whether you agree or not, I felt it had to be done.''

She turned and went outside.

Mike moved to the window and watched her walk away. Why was he so hard on her? He understood where she was coming from. He'd do the same thing in her position. So why couldn't he be more patient with her?

Because he was scared, that's why. Scared something would happen to her. That he'd fail to protect her. But she was wrong about something: it had nothing to do with his reputation. He was damn scared for her. Whoever was behind this rotten situation had connections all over the place. There was no place they could go—no place he could take her—that they wouldn't eventually be discovered.

No place he could keep her safe.

There was a lot he'd like to say to her. She had grit and courage. He really admired those traits—if only she'd stop self-destructing. And he sure as hell wanted her physically. The need for her had been chewing on his groin from the first time he looked at her. Now it had become more than just chemistry between a man and woman. His emotions had crept into it, too, and he knew the moment he touched her it'd be curtains for sure. He had to hold on to his objectivity. Not foul up his mind with personal feelings, because the only hope he had to keep her alive was to stay one step ahead of whoever was after her.

Against his better judgment he'd lowered his guard and made the mistake of agreeing to let her go back to work. Well, he wouldn't make that mistake again.

His gaze followed her as she sat down on the end of the pier. If anybody was going to get to her it sure as hell would have to be through him, because from now on he wasn't going to let her out of his sight 24/7. She might end up hating the sight of him…*but he wouldn't make that mistake again.*

Chapter 21

Ann was still sitting on the end of the pier when Mike came outside. "Let's go. I have to go to town."

"Can't I stay here?"

"No!" He hadn't intended to sound so abrupt, but it came out that way. Grinning, he softened his tone. "Besides, there must be some items you need. My cabin isn't equipped for female occupancy." As he clasped her hand and pulled her to her feet, Mike felt a powerful surge of sensation from the warmth of her touch. Without intent, he held its softness longer than necessary, and she pulled her hand away.

"I'm tired, Mike. I'd much rather stay here and rest."

"You'll have plenty of time to rest when we get back."

He unlocked the shed and wheeled out a motorcycle. "Here, put this on," he said, handing her a helmet.

Her eyes widened with shock. "You expect me to ride on that?"

"You ever ride on the back of a bike before?"

"I'm proud to say I haven't, and I don't intend to start now." She shoved the helmet into his hands and spun on her heel to walk away. His hand gripped her arm before she could even take a step.

"Hamilton, don't give me an argument. You've done enough damage for one day. I have to go to town, and I'm not leaving you alone."

She expelled a deep sigh and turned to face him. "I hate motorcycles. They scare me, Mike. They're loud and dangerous."

"Did you ever ride a bicycle, Ann?"

"When I was young."

"Well they're easier and safer than riding a bicycle. And they're not dangerous if you obey the rules of the road and don't try to be another Evel Knievel."

He put the helmet on her head and tightened the strap under her chin. Then he mounted the seat. "Climb on."

The seat narrowed to a small pad at the rear. With reservation she straddled it. "What do I hold on to?"

"Me," he said. She grabbed him around the waist when he revved up the motor, and they took off.

The narrow road leading to his cabin was bumpy and unpaved, and she clung to him. Once they reached the highway, the five-mile ride into town was smooth.

She couldn't believe the number of people in the quaint town. Rhinelander was a popular resort area and was swarming with tourists. Mike spent a few minutes talking to the garage mechanic, then he took her hand and they faded inconspicuously into the crowd.

They went into a pharmacy so he could call Waterman. As much as she yearned to call Brandon, Mike had forbidden her to make any contact with the boy. Her heart ached thinking of the child's unhappiness and knew he'd be more miserable than ever when he didn't hear from her.

As she waited for Mike to finish his call, Ann bought a

half dozen hygiene articles, decided she might as well put her idle time to use by taking pictures and bought several more rolls of film and flash bulbs.

"All set?" Mike asked when he rejoined her.

"I could use a swimming suit. That lake looked very inviting."

"Okay, but make it quick."

They ducked into one of the many souvenir shops and the only one she could find in her size was a blue bikini. It was skimpier than she'd normally wear, but with Mike waiting impatiently she knew it would have to be this one or none at all.

When they returned to the garage, the black shiny motorcycle was loaded on the back of a beat-up old pick-up truck that looked like something out of *The Grapes of Wrath.*

"Yours?" she asked.

He nodded. "Comes in handy when I need it. I garage it here when I'm gone."

He opened the front door of the cab. "Your carriage awaits, madam."

She snapped her finger. "Darn! Just when I was looking forward to bouncing around on the back of that motorcycle again."

"You want bounce, lady. Just wait. The shocks are really shot on this truck. I've been meaning to have them replaced."

"You're so good to me, Bishop." She climbed in, and he had to slam the door several times to get it to stay closed. Remarkably, the door didn't fall off.

Much to her surprise, the engine turned over and purred contentedly as soon as he turned on the ignition.

Mike smiled smugly. "You see. Never judge a book by its cover, Hamilton. I can push this baby up to 110 if I have to."

"No doubt, Bishop. But the tires fall off then, right?"

"Lady, that's so not so." He shifted into gear, and the truck rolled smoothly down the road.

"What about groceries?" she asked.

"Cassidy took care of that earlier, but if you want, we can run through the store and check it out."

"I want," she said. Anything was better than going back to that cabin. Right now they were getting along well, but there was a lot of daylight remaining, and based on past experience she knew that when left on their own it invariably led to another argument.

Ann glanced askance at him. "Dare I ask where Cassidy went?"

"Can't stop you from asking."

By now she'd come to learn that kind of answer was the only one she was going to get. He was so predictable.

They stopped at a supermarket, and Ann went up and down each aisle selecting an item here and there. Mike pushed the cart and would occasionally toss an item into the basket.

"We're not going to be at the cabin long enough to eat all this," he grumbled when they left the store loaded down with two heaping bags full of groceries. "Dave loaded us up pretty good earlier."

"We didn't buy that many perishables. You can always store the rest for next time."

"If there is a next time."

The comment was too portentous to ignore. For a short time she had actually forgotten about the situation they were in.

Welcome back to the real world, Ann.

"Are you paranoid, Mike?" she asked, trying to avoid hitting her head against the cab's roof as they bounced back to the cabin.

He threw her a quick glance. "Why do you ask?"

"Every time we go somewhere we start out in one vehicle and return in a different one. In Kourou we used several different ones. In England we rode in a limo and a Ferrari. Today we left the cabin in a motorcycle and are returning in a broken-down pick-up truck. Does this pattern have something to do with your choice of professions?"

He laughed. "I'm told that variety is the spice of life."

"Yes, but you take it to a new high."

"Be honest, Hamilton. You're just disappointed because you didn't get to ride back on the bike."

"That, too," she said. They looked at each other and burst into laughter.

She felt good. Indeed, the whole mood between them had changed. They both relaxed, and as soon as they unpacked the groceries, Mike suggested a swim.

The suit she had purchased was even more revealing than she had thought. The skimpy pants called for a knot on each side to keep them on. The top was nothing more than a narrow strip that knotted in back to keep it in place. How one could swim in it without dislodging either piece would be a challenge, but she was determined to try. Trouble was, she couldn't reach to tie a secure knot behind her back, and she'd have to get Mike's help.

He had changed into swimming trunks and was waiting on the pier.

"Will you help me with this?" she asked, clutching the top of the bikini across her breasts.

He took one look at her and gaped. "Wow!"

She felt herself actually blush under the appreciative gaze sweeping her from head to toe. "You're going to be adult about this, aren't you, Mike? I would very much like to have a pleasant swim."

"I'll try, Hamilton, to be very adult. But it's sure going to be hard."

"So I've noticed," she said in amusement with a quick glance at the bulge in his trunks. "Just tie this for me then you can jump in the lake and cool off."

"Well, this is a twist," he said as he knotted the ends of the bikini top.

No doubt it was. He more then likely was used to untying a woman's top rather than tying one. Since the conversation was getting a little risqué, she thought it wiser to play dumb and innocent.

"No, don't twist the ends, Mike. Tie them together in a knot."

"That's what I'm trying to do, lady, but my hands are shaking. You knock the legs out from under a guy. You've got one great face and body, Hamilton. You should be in front of the camera, not behind it."

"I can say the same about you, Mike. You'd make a great model, and could probably make a lot more money than what you're getting now. And less risky, too—you'd only have to fight off sex-crazed females. Think it over, Mike." She dove into the water.

It felt good to strike out and work the muscles in her arms and legs. She'd always been a good swimmer. Had swum competitively in high school and college. But even though Mike slowed his strokes, she couldn't keep up with the ex-Navy SEAL who was as at home in the water as he was on land. After several rigorous laps, she settled back to just romping and splashing like a child in the refreshing water.

She finally got out and lay down on the pier to dry off. Mike climbed out and stretched out on his stomach beside her with his head resting on his folded arms.

"That felt good," she said.

"Yeah."

"It's beautiful up here, Mike. How long have you had this place?"

"About ten years."

"Why here."

"My Dad was RA until he joined the CIA and—"

"RA?" she asked.

"Regular army. He was a professional soldier so we lived in a lot of different bases and countries. But whenever my folks had the chance, we'd come to vacation in this area. Dad joined the CIA when I was sixteen, and then we never came back after that. But I couldn't get the place out of my mind. Guess I've come to think of this area as my roots even though I was born in Milwaukee."

"Must be because the area holds pleasant memories for you."

"Guess it does. It sure did for Mom. Dad was all hers up here. Not the army's. And he was Dad to me, not Captain Bishop."

"Did you resent his military career, Mike?"

"Guess I did at the time. As I grew older, I came to see it through different eyes. I'm proud of him. He devoted his adult life to serving his country."

She wished she had her camera at that moment to catch the look of pride in his eyes when he spoke of his father.

She had so misjudged him in the past. Mike was really a very remarkable individual. He had the character to turn around what obviously had been childhood resentment toward his father—which very well could have destroyed his own adult life if he'd allowed himself to obsess on it—into a sense of pride, honor and love of country that drove him to follow in his father's footsteps.

"Isn't it rather secluded for someone who lives in the fast lane like you?"

"Seclusion's good," he said.

"Did you ever think about marriage? A family?"

"Yeah, I thought about it—thought what a bad idea it would be."

"I don't think you're as cynical as you'd like people to believe."

"Don't go soft on me, Hamilton. You've just seen the tip of the iceberg."

"So you've said. Is that your standard reply to frighten off women?"

"What do you think?"

The conversation was going down a dangerous road. She stood up. "I think I'm thirsty. Should I bring you something?"

"Yeah, a beer."

When she came back, he had fallen asleep. She looked at him stretched out on the pier. He had such a beautifully developed body that she couldn't resist looking at him. Broad shoulders, slim hips and long, muscular legs. His flesh was firm. Muscular and firm. Not the overdeveloped corded muscles and physique of the muscle-bound apes who competed for titles. Mike's physique reflected a man who used his muscles, not merely displayed them.

She hurried back into the house and grabbed her camera.

Ann had only taken a half dozen pictures when he raised his head. "What do you think you're doing?"

"I couldn't resist all that bronzed brawn, Bishop."

"I told you, no pictures."

"Come on, Mike. Let me take a few. I'm willing to pay you for posing."

"There's not enough money, lady. In my business, anonymity is the best weapon. I don't need my face plastered all over some damn magazine."

"But it's such a beautiful face, Mike. I promise I won't use them professionally. I'll just keep a couple."

"What for?"

That sounded a little encouraging. Maybe he was breaking down. "To remember you by. So how about it, Mike?"

"Fair enough, if you'll let me take a few of you."

"Me?"

"Sure. To remember *you* by," he said.

"Now why would you want to remember me, Bishop? I'm your nemesis. A royal pain in your posterior. You've told me that enough times."

"Actually, that's not true anymore," he said.

"Well thank you, Mike. I'm flattered. Does this mean you've decided I'm not so bad after all?"

He never cracked a smile. "No, it means that the pain's done a 180-degree turn."

It took her several seconds to grasp the innuendo.

"So if I go along with your terms, do you agree to pose the way I want you to?" she asked.

"This was your idea, not mine, so don't try putting me on the defensive."

"Okay. We've got a deal," she said.

Ann got several more pictures of him in his swimming suit on the pier, and he took one of her. By that time it had turned dark, and they moved inside for indoor shots. He changed into jeans and a muscle shirt. After taking several more shots she went into the bedroom to change the film and put the flash attachment on the camera.

When she came back, Mike had opened a bottle of wine. In between shots they drank wine and munched on cheese and crackers.

She then had him remove the muscle shirt and got a great shot of him straddling a chair with his arms draped over the back of it. Took another one of him leaning against the doorjamb in the kitchen with his arms folded across his chest. She caught a candid shot of his back as he stood and looked out the window, then posed him with his foot propped on the seat of a chair and his arm draped casually over his bent knee.

"Do you have a long-sleeved white shirt?" she asked.

"Yeah."

"Put it on."

He grimaced. "You mean with a tie?"

"No, just leave the shirt unbuttoned."

"How many more of these stupid poses are you going to take?" he asked when he came out of the bedroom. "I thought you wanted shots of my beautiful face."

"Well, that bod is just as beautiful," she said. "Roll the sleeves up to your elbows, lean across the countertop and look at the camera.

"Okay, now let's concentrate on your face," she said. "Who's the sexiest woman you can think of?"

His expression became seductive, an invitation in his half-closed eyes. She felt a heated flush and suddenly found it hard to concentrate on what she was doing.

"That's great, Mike. I bet you don't have a problem remembering *her* name. So keep that thought and unfasten your jeans and slide them just a tad down more toward your hips."

"I don't know what you mean," he said, with a crafty gleam in his eye.

She went over to him and adjusted the jean's fly to her liking. In the course of it, her hand inadvertently brushed against the restrained bulge in his pants. He was aroused, and the thought of it was raising her excitement. This whole thing was turning her on as much as it was him.

She paused and emptied her wineglass, then once again angled the camera and snapped it.

"You know, Bishop, if we ever made these pictures into a calendar, you could make some big bucks."

"And become the laughing stock of the Agency."

"Hold the pose, but this time hook your thumbs in your waistband," she said. "And think of that woman again."

He did, and the picture she got could set asbestos on fire. "Who is she, Mike?"

"You."

Ann almost dropped her camera. "Whew, it's getting quite hot in here."

"Really? And you dressed only in that bikini! They say if you can't stand the heat get out of the kitchen. Kitchen getting too hot, Hamilton?" he taunted.

He was flinging a blatant challenge at her. The sexual attraction both of them had been fighting had reached a tension that lay on the air like humidity—so heavy it was an effort to breathe.

"If you can stand it so can I," she said.

"Don't make book on that, baby. Now, if you're through, it's my turn."

Chapter 22

Ann handed him the camera. "Do you know how to use it?"

"No problem." He stroked his chin as he studied her. "Hmm, how do I want to remember you?"

"Should I change into something other than this swimming suit?" she asked.

"No, suit's fine. How about kneeling down, Ann? Tuck those gorgeous legs under you, and rest that trim little tush of yours on them."

It was a pose she had used often with models, so she knew immediately what he was looking for.

He came over to her. "Now lets get rid of these stupid pins," he said. He pulled them out and when her hair dropped in long coils to her shoulders, he brushed the tresses apart with his fingers. "That's better." He stepped back to admire the effect. "Now remove the top of your bikini."

"No way! You never said anything about nudity."

"And you never said anything against nudity, so that makes it a moot issue. You even said a naked human body is beautiful, Ann. And you had to know I don't want this picture to hang on the door of a locker room."

"Maybe not, but that doesn't mean you won't share it with your buddies."

"Ann. I don't kiss and tell. I promise you the picture is for my eyes only. My word is my bond."

Normally she still wouldn't have accepted that argument, but maybe it was the wine she'd drunk, the excitement of the moment—or maybe even that Stockholm Syndrome kicking up its heels—whatever the reason, she felt daring enough to do it.

She untied the knot and pulled the top off. The instant the air hit her nipples, they changed into taut peaks. She had the satisfaction of seeing him suck in his breath.

"I can say unequivocally, lady, you've got one beautiful pair of—"

"Get on with it, Bishop. No doubt you've done plenty of personal research on the subject."

She did feel beautiful, though. Although what she was doing was against her personal conduct code, on occasion as a favor to some of the models who asked in the past she had taken nude shots for them to give to their husbands or sweethearts.

And she did believe in the beauty of the human body and did not look upon photographing it as pornography, any more than an artist or sculptor did when fashioning it on canvas or clay.

But her reason for posing bare-chested for Mike went beyond that. They'd set a juggernaut in motion tonight. She felt a high in letting Mike do this. A total abandonment of modesty and inhibition that created a sensual excitement that had nothing to do with artistry, but more with simply being male and female. She smiled slyly. He admired her body—and she was damn glad he did.

The click of the camera captured that expression.

"Now one in the bedroom," he said.

She followed him to the bedside and he turned to her. She snagged his arm when he began to tug at the knot of her bikini bottoms. She looked up into the tawny hazel of his eyes, and for a long moment their gazes locked. Then he put into words what both of them were thinking.

"It's too late to turn back now," he said.

She didn't—couldn't—answer, because he was right. Slowly she withdrew her hand from his arm. He released the knot and she felt the cool slide of the bikini brush against the heat of her naked thigh.

Oh, he was very good with knots. Very swift. They held no challenge to him. Within the blink of an eye the other knot gave way and the pants dropped to the floor. Only then did he break their fixed stare. His gaze slowly swept the length of her before he picked up the camera and moved to the foot of the bed.

"Get on the bed, Ann, and stretch out on your back."

She felt no modesty. No self-consciousness. Nudity was commonplace in today's society. Fashion, movies, television, commercials all thrived on marketing the human body as naked as they could get away with.

But this was her body. And in the privacy of his bedroom the situation was too intimate, the desire that was raging between them too intense. Indifference was impossible. She became drugged with aroused passion.

"Raise your arms a little above each side of your face and crook them at the elbows," he said.

She'd often used the pose he wanted, only, the model was usually lying on satin sheets wearing a filmy piece of expensive lingerie.

He came back to the bedside and stared down at her

with those sensuous bedroom eyes. His had to be the pro-
totype for whoever coined the damn phrase.

She lay open and exposed as his smoldering gaze now
raked her boldly with no attempt at indifference. He was
photographing her with his eyes and not the camera.

The nipples of her breasts were taut; her heart a deafening thumping in her chest; and the core of her sex was
throbbing like a coiled spring being wound tighter and
tighter until it was on the verge of popping. She shifted,
anxiously. She was so far gone she ached for him.

Touch me, Mike. Touch me, she pleaded silently. She
had to feel his hands on her—his mouth—or she'd go out
of her mind. What was he waiting for? At the moment
she'd be willing to do anything he asked—if only he would
touch her.

She closed her eyes with expectation when he raised a
hand and reached toward her, then opened them in bafflement when all he did was fan her hair out on the pillow,
and then return to the foot of the bed.

For God's sake, Mike, take the damn picture! There was
no disguising her arousal. He knew what he was doing to
her. Was he playing a cat-and-mouse game with her?

"Now, close your eyes, Ann, and think of what you
want me to do to you when I finish with this shot."

He was in complete control and knew it. But she was
too aroused to care. She'd surrendered her control the moment she'd given in and removed her bikini top.

Her body felt flushed, her breasts heavy, swelling with
each breath that had begun to come in gasps as her aroused
passion spiraled into raw lust. She thought of how his
hands would feel against her nakedness, his mouth on her
breasts, his tongue on her sex. Yes, she wanted it all now.
Anything and everything. He hadn't kissed her or even
touched her yet, but he'd driven her to the point where she
wanted it all—where anything goes.

Her lips and throat felt parched from the swirling heat within her. She could barely swallow. Parting her lips, she moistened them with her tongue and opened her eyes, the lids so heavy with passion she could barely raise them.

He snapped his shot.

"Hurry, Mike. Please hurry," she implored.

He had already put aside the camera and was at the bedside. Her eyes pleaded with him as he shed his jeans in one smooth movement. Then he was on her. His weight pressed gloriously against her with a velvet friction as his mouth and tongue feasted on her lips and breasts.

She had fantasized this moment from the first time they met—the arousal of his touch, the thrill of his kiss—until the thought had become obsessive. But the expectation did not come near the exquisite sensation of the actual moment.

All the arguing between them had been the foreplay, and there was no necessity for more. Her body was ready for him, and imploded with tremors the instant he touched her. And as quickly as they passed over her, his mouth and hands aroused her to a moaning plea for more.

The slight pause when he put on protection was an unwelcome exercise in restraint, until she felt the heated, throbbing hardness of him slide into her, the ecstatic soar to mindlessness and then the rapturous tremors of climax.

He rolled off her and she lay in the afterglow knowing this moment would be etched on her mind forever. Nothing or no one could ever duplicate it.

No doubt there were other men as accomplished at making love as Mike Bishop. But what they had just shared went beyond being the greatest sex she had ever known, and there was no fooling herself about the reason why.

She was hopelessly in love with Mike Bishop.

Love had brought a whole new element to sex that she'd never experienced before. Oh, she had thought she was in love a couple of times in the past, but something had always caused her to recognize that it wasn't really love. So she had walked away from the relationships.

Love had been the missing excitement in the sex she had with them—the missing ingredient that had made this so incredible. It was as if it was the first time, and to her way of thinking, it was. It could never happen again—even with Mike.

She doubted he loved her. But she wouldn't allow that to spoil the moment. After all, he did desire her. Had told her as much when they were in New York. And it would be his decision if this was to be a one-night stand, because she was too much in love with him to be able to walk away from this relationship willingly.

He'd been so right when he said they'd come too far to stop now. She had herself to blame for putting it all in motion when she started taking pictures of him. But she had no regrets. She'd have this moment forever.

He turned on his side, propped up an elbow and cradled his head in his hand. Reaching out, he brushed some errant strands of hair off her cheek.

"Regrets, Ann?"

She turned her head and looked up into those mesmerizing hazel eyes of his. "Why would you think that?"

"Because you know as well as I that this was a mistake."

"Then you're the one with regrets."

"I don't regret making love to you, Ann."

"Then why is it a mistake?"

"Because of the timing. Your life is in danger and—"

"Hush," she said, putting the tips of her fingers over his lips. "Let's not spoil what we just shared with talk of danger."

He kissed her fingertips, then she felt the tantalizing warmth of his touch when he cupped her cheek with the palm of his hand. "I won't let anything happen to you, Ann."

"Whatever happens, we still have tonight, Mike."

"I thought you didn't believe in one-night stands, Violet Eyes," he murmured between light nibbles at her lips.

"And I thought you didn't believe in mixing business and pleasure, Agent Bishop," she retorted, trying to sound serious when her heart was overflowing with love and her body beginning to respond to him. Even the huskiness of his voice was a turn-on to her.

"We're a real pair, aren't we? We sure have wasted a lot of time trying to hold on to good intentions."

She clasped her arms around his neck. "Then, let's not waste another minute."

He shifted closer, slipped his arms beneath her and drew her tightly into his embrace. He felt long and hard, strong and exciting. The dark hair on his chest rasped against the sensitive peaks of her breasts in a tantalizing sensation that sent shivers down her spine. His kiss clouded her brain with the thrilling turbulence of passion.

Mike was a great lover and aroused her with slow, erotic kisses. She marveled at the intensity of her own response. Passion flowed through her in a floodtide whenever his hands joined the seduction.

She loved the feel of his hands. They were warm and gentle as they caressed and explored her. And she reveled in wanton response to the touch of them.

They made love throughout the night. Dozing, waking. Hot and passionate. Slow and gentle. There were times they simply caressed, kissed or merely reached out to touch each other. But every kiss, tender touch or whispered endearment drew her deeper and deeper into an emotional response as intense as the physical one.

And her intuition told her she'd passed the point of no

return—she could never willingly leave this man. Which caused her to ponder whether he felt the same about her.

Mike woke up with a start. Bright sunlight streamed through the open window. He glanced at his watch and saw that it was nine o'clock. He jumped out of bed. Good Lord! He'd slept through half of the morning with the windows wide open and no one on guard. Anyone could have gotten in and cut their throats.

He glanced at Ann asleep in the bed. For a brief moment his expression softened as he gazed at her. She looked so at peace as she slept.

Turning away quickly, he pulled on his jeans, cursing himself for the idiot he was. Because he couldn't keep his hands off her—and his pants on—he very well could have gotten her killed.

He'd never been this careless before. He'd lost his objectivity completely and allowed his personal feelings for her to interfere with the performance of his duty.

He went outside on the porch and glanced around. Everything was peaceful and quiet. He sensed that all was okay for the moment.

Closing the barn after the horses were out. The thought produced another string of self-deprecating curses.

He leaned back against the porch wall. So he'd dodged the bullet again, but that didn't excuse last night's negligence.

Even though he figured no one would show up until tomorrow, or late tonight at the earliest, he'd been trained to be prepared for the unexpected. Well Mr. Unknown was in for a little surprise himself when Cassidy got back with the guys. He was through running. Hiding away in hotels to try and protect her. It wasn't his way of fighting. He was in Special Ops. They took the fight to their enemies— not the other way around.

He wished Ann wasn't in the line of fire. But there was no place where he'd be certain she'd be safe. When you were fighting an unknown enemy, the only thing you could put your trust in was your team.

"Good morning," Ann said, coming outside.

"Hi."

"Hope you don't mind. I found this pajama top in a drawer."

He took a long look at her. Her hair was disheveled and the pajama top looked better on her than it ever would on him. She looked good. Damn good. Of course, she always looked good. But she could never look better to him than she had last night. He would never get the image of how she looked lying naked on his bed out of his mind. The thought of it began licking at his groin. He was getting hard, and the guilty conscience he'd been struggling with only moments before had just become the last thing on his mind.

"I wouldn't have thought you were the pajama type, Bishop," she said lightly. She rose on tiptoe and kissed him on the cheek.

She smelled of toothpaste and the faint fragrance of that perfume he'd bought her. And she smelled of woman.

"I'm not. They were a Christmas gift from my mom years ago. Can't remember ever wearing them."

He had to touch her, so he put his hand on the thigh of one of her long, tanned legs sticking out from beneath the top. He thought of the gorgeous breasts concealed under it, the satin flesh, and he slid his hand higher. He could feel the ends of her nerves jumping under his touch. She felt so good. Warm. Satiny. Responsive. So damn responsive.

His hormones took over. Once again his brain shifted down to between his legs, and he picked her up and carried her into the bedroom.

Chapter 23

Later they showered together—his contribution to water conservation. He rejected the washcloth and used his hands to soap her, while she did the same to him. By the time they finished, they both were so aroused they made love in the shower.

The mood continued throughout most of the day. They swam, lazed in the sun and made love off and on. It was dusk by the time hunger forced them to finally dress and prepare something to eat. He watched her as she scrambled eggs and fried bacon. He enjoyed finally being able to openly stare at her as she moved around him.

"Supper's ready," she said, when she finished.

"You may call it supper, but I consider it breakfast," he said.

"Mike, it's 6 p.m., not a.m."

"I don't read you," he said. "Did we eat breakfast earlier?"

"Well no, but—"

"Then, what's the first meal of the day? Breakfast."

"But it's past breakfast and lunchtime, so it's supper."

"Maybe to you, but I intend to eat my *supper* later. I weighed myself and I've lost a pound. Either I've missed too many meals in the past couple of days, or I've screwed it off since last night."

"Michael, please don't be crude while we're eating."

"Crude? I thought I'd cleaned it up." He grinned boyishly, "Want to wash my mouth out with soap, Mama?"

"That's an appealing thought," she said.

"Yeah, sure is. Maybe we should get back under that shower."

"Do you ever stop thinking about sex?"

"I heard a statistic that men think about it every ten seconds," he said.

"Is that collectively or in shifts?" she asked.

He chuckled. "You're such a smart as—" he choked back the word "—ah...as you can be, Hamilton."

"Smart enough to know if we don't change this subject, we'll never get out of here. Didn't you say you have to go into town?"

"Right. We better think about getting out of here."

"At least in the next ten seconds," she said. She grabbed her plate and hurried to the sink with Mike in hot pursuit.

She washed, he dried the dishes and within ten minutes they were on their way.

"What do you have to go to town for?" she asked as they bounced along in the Ford pickup. "I thought we did all our shopping yesterday."

"I have to call Waterman. Unless you have something specifically that you need we don't even have to go all the way into town. I'm coming up on a motel near the outskirts. There's a telephone booth there."

"Fine with me. I don't need anything in particular," she said.

As he dialed Waterman at the Agency, the scream of sirens shattered the quiet afternoon as an ambulance and police car raced up the road and turned in at the motel. Waterman's private line didn't answer, so Mike left word on the voice mail and hung up. At least Waterman couldn't accuse him again of keeping him out of the loop.

Seeing the arrival of another police car, and a crowd of people standing around gaping, curiosity got the better of him and he walked over to a nearby couple.

"What happened?" he asked.

"The maid found a dead man in one of the rooms," the man said.

"That's too bad." He started to turn away when the woman said, "He was murdered." Her eyes were wide with alarm. "I bet someone robbed him."

Mike stopped and glanced at the man. "Murdered? How do they know he was murdered?" The man made a cutting motion across his neck.

"We all could have been slaughtered in our sleep," the agitated woman said.

"What's going on?" Ann asked, appearing suddenly at his side.

"Didn't I tell you to stay in the truck?"

"I'm just as curious as you are," she said. "What happened?"

"I guess some guy was murdered."

The murmurs among the crowd quieted as the ambulance crew rolled out a black body bag on a gurney and loaded it into the ambulance. The vehicle raced away with siren screaming.

The crowd started to disperse and return to their rooms, and for the first time Mike had a full view of the white

Camero parked in front of the open door of the unit where the body had been found. His intuition kicked in when he saw a Milwaukee dealer's license plate on the car. He quickly scoped the crowd but didn't recognize one of them.

"Anybody know who he was?" he asked.

The man shook his head and pointed to a man speaking with one of the officers. "That's the motel manager talking to the sheriff. He can probably tell you."

"Ann, get back into the truck. *Now!*" he declared when she hesitated. She had the good sense to recognize that he meant business. As soon as she climbed into the cab and closed the door, he pretended to appear curious like the other bystanders who had remained at the scene, and moseyed near enough to the manager and sheriff to eavesdrop on their conversation.

"You say this DeVilles checked in a short time ago?" the sheriff said.

"Yeah, not more than an hour."

"Was he alone?"

"Said he was, but my wife saw another man in the car."

"Where is he from?"

"He put down Milwaukee. That's his car, but you can see it ain't his. It's a rental."

"Check it out," the sheriff said to one of the officers. "And let's have a look at that registration book." The two men went into the motel lobby.

Mike hurried back to the truck. "We've got a problem." He dug some coins out of his jeans pocket. "Dammit! I need some more change."

"I have a lot of change," she said, and pulled out her change purse and grabbed a handful. "What do you need?"

"A quarter."

She handed him a fistful of coins and he hurried to the

phone booth. Time had become critical. Digging out a quarter, he shoved the rest of the coins into his pocket.

Dave Cassidy answered his cell phone before it could ring twice.

"We've got a problem here," Mike said. He kept his gaze trained on Ann in the truck.

"So what else is new?" Cassidy said, cynically.

"Ricardo DeVilles's dead body just turned up here with a ventilated throat."

Cassidy whistled. "Sounds like your suspicions about him were right."

"That means the killer's here already."

"If DeVilles was a party to the conspiracy, why was he killed?" Cassidy asked.

"I don't know. Just hurry. I've got to get Ann back to the cabin."

"Where are you now?"

"In a phone booth of a motel near town."

"Why don't you stay there until we arrive?"

"Too many people around. I can't watch them all. Is the squad with you?"

"Yeah. We're about an hour away," Cassidy said.

"Hurry."

Mike hung up and ran back to the truck.

"What's going on, Mike?" Ann asked.

"Hold on to your seat, baby. They just wheeled out the dead body of your friend DeVilles." He pushed the truck to ninety.

"Ricardo's dead! What...how?"

"He was murdered."

"Murdered!" The color drained from her face, and those violet eyes of hers looked even deeper and darker against the pallor as they glistened with tears.

"Don't waste tears on him, baby. He was into this mess up to his eyebrows."

"You don't know that, Mike," she murmured sadly. "You didn't really know him."

She sounded on the verge of breaking into sobs, but was fighting to hold on to her control. She had a lot of grit—and even now loyalty to a bastard Mike was convinced didn't deserve it.

"Then whoever is trying to kill me is here now," she said.

"You've got that right."

"Why go back to the cabin? Why don't we just keep driving?"

He understood her desperation. He was feeling it, too. He forced himself to stay focused.

"Ann, honey, there comes a time when we have to stop running and hiding. This guy's too cunning. We've got to face him and take him down."

"You don't know how many others are with him. You can't do it alone."

"I know that. The squad should be here within an hour. Cassidy picked them up in Milwaukee."

He screeched to a stop in the yard. "Get inside," he shouted, and hurried her into the house. "Keep the lights off. It'll soon be dark, and there's no sense in making us easy targets. If there's any shooting, flatten yourself on the floor."

Ann looked more scared now than he'd ever seen her. He wanted to take her in his arms and assure her she'd be safe. That he'd never let anyone harm her.

But right now they were racing the clock, and every minute was vital. He checked the rear door to make sure it was locked, then bolted the shutters on all the windows except for a couple in the living room to enable him to scan the front yard. He closed and locked the bedroom door shoved the couch against the front door, and then lifted a heavy armchair on top to reinforce it.

Ann had watched him with disbelief. She was growing more frightened by the minute.

"Mike, you're acting like you're expecting a siege."

"If there's more than one, I can't cover every door and window in the house. I'm just narrowing the perimeter. Now just sit down and relax. We'll wait this out."

"Do you have any idea who might have murdered Ricardo?"

"It's got to come down to who knew where to find you. Tell me the truth, Ann, did you make any contact with DeVilles since we returned from Kourou?"

"No, Mike. I swear it."

"What about Brandon?"

She shook her head. "As much as I wanted to, I didn't."

"That means, then, the only people we know for sure who knew where you were was your boss, the Agency and the guys on my squad."

"Mike, I know Barney would never do anything that could harm me."

"Well, not intentionally," Mike said.

"Or unintentionally. Barney wouldn't say anything to someone he doesn't know well enough to trust. Besides, I never actually told Barney where I was when I called him. He only knew that I was back in the United States."

"Well, I can rule out any member of my squad. We've been through too much together."

"But no one's trying to kill you, Mike. It's me they're after."

"Ann, don't even think it. I know every one of those guys. We're like brothers."

"Well then what about the CIA?"

"Give it up, Ann. Waterman and Baker are the two honchos working this case, and they're trying to save you, not harm you."

"Yes, but what about their assistants or secretaries? Maybe one of them could have leaked something."

"Employees who work for the people at the level of Baker and Waterman have usually gone through pretty tough security checks to get the job. And besides that, you can rule out Baker's staff. They're out of the loop. He's been on leave for the past week same as the squad. The last time I talked to him was the day he asked me to go to England with you. On top of that, you need motive. Waterman's retiring the end of this year, and Baker's been with the Agency since 'Nam."

He sat down at the table, checked his gun, then emptied his pockets and stuffed the gun clips he had into them.

"Is there something I can do to be useful?" she asked.

"Just stay calm, honey. You're doing great."

She sat down beside him and glanced at the pile of change she'd given him. "Oh, my goodness!"

Ann picked up one of the coins about the size of a silver dollar. "I forgot to give this back to Brandon when I laundered his pajamas. He cherishes it. His grandfather gave him the coin the last time they were together."

"Must be valuable," Mike said.

"I don't think so. It's just an English commemorative coin honoring the British queen and her mother."

Mike picked it up and studied it. The front was a profile of Queen Elizabeth II.

"You say Burroughs gave this to the kid?"

Ann nodded. "Yes, the very morning he was killed."

He turned it over. It had been coined August 4, 1980, and the engraving read, "QUEEN ELIZABETH THE QUEEN MOTHER."

"Oh, my God!" Mike exclaimed. "I can't believe it! And it's been right under our noses the whole time. Queen Mother is the Agency's code name for Avery Waterman." He grabbed his cell phone and dialed Cassidy.

"Dave, Waterman is the one behind this."

Chapter 24

A burst of bullets ripped the house, blowing out the windows. Mike dropped the phone and threw himself at Ann. Knocking her to the floor, he sprawled across her and tried to protect her.

"Dammit! He's got an AK-47." He'd been in combat enough to recognize the sound, and once you heard it, you didn't forget it. His pistol would be worthless against the Russian-made assault weapon.

"Stay down," he whispered, shoving Ann under the table. Clutching his pistol, he crawled over to the window just as another burst rattled the truck, blowing out the tires and windows.

"The son of a bitch is shooting up my truck," he said. "Give it up, Waterman," he shouted. "It's too late. We've got your number."

"It's not going to do you any good when you're dead, Agent Bishop," Waterman called back.

"I've already called the Agency."

''Good try, Bishop, but I don't think so.'' Another burst hit the fuel tank, and the truck exploded.

''That was stupid, Waterman. That explosion and fire will attract attention. The fire department will be out here soon.''

''Not before they can do you any good. I'll be long gone by then.'' He raked the house again with gunfire.

''Or long dead,'' Mike shouted, returning his fire. ''Ann, we've got to get out of here,'' he whispered. ''It won't be long before he figures he can drive us out by exploding the gas tank. While I keep him occupied, crawl to the back door and unlock it. He's obviously alone or we'd be taking fire from elsewhere. I doubt he knows about the motorcycle or he would have shot up the tires on that, too. If we can get into the woods, he'll follow us. With luck we can double back and get away on the bike.

''Waterman,'' he shouted, ''how about a deal?''

''What kind of a deal?''

''We both know my pistol's worthless against your assault weapon, so you've got the advantage.''

Waterman's laughter was as piercing as one of those cartridges he was firing at them. ''What did you expect, Agent Bishop, a two-man face-off on the street in the center of the town? Sorry, old chap, John Wayne's dead.''

''Listen to me, Waterman.'' He motioned to Ann to get moving. ''I lied to you. The Agency doesn't know about you, so it's not too late. What's the sense of us killing each other?''

''You saying you'll turn the woman over to me?''

''I might, if you make it worth my while.''

Waterman broke into more laughter. ''It won't work, Bishop. We've worked together too long for me to fall for that ploy. You're too 'Stars and Stripes Forever' to give up on a mission. Sorry, old chap, but I'm afraid I'll have to kill you.''

Mike fired several return shots and while Waterman sprayed the house again with gunshots, he crawled across the floor. Ann was out the door and he caught up with her, grabbed her by the hand, and they dashed into the woods.

A spray of bullets kicked up the dirt at their feet just as they reached the trees. Fortunately this forest was thick with growth, with much better cover to conceal them, unlike the shelter they had sought in the copse of trees in Kourou. Unfortunately they weren't out of the range of Waterman's rifle, and if he caught sight of them, he'd be able to pick them off.

Mike purposely headed toward the road leading to the highway. If they were serious about escaping, Waterman would expect them to try to get to the highway where the possibility of encountering traffic would be feasible.

But darkness was where Mike was in his element. He'd been trained to remain in the shadows and operate in a hostile environment where the enemy had everything in his favor.

Waterman had the superior weapon to his advantage, but had been long out of the field and would have to have lost some of his edge. Mike's disadvantage was Ann. He had her to protect, which prevented him attempting anything difficult like he would on a mission with his squad.

Ann was a good runner, so he let it become a foot race for about half a mile. When he drew Waterman far enough away from the cabin, he reversed his direction and turned to stealth.

They moved carefully through the woods trying to avoid rustling a leaf or breaking a twig. Occasionally they'd spot a deer, but not the chirp of a cricket or twitter of a bird broke the silence.

Then Mike suddenly stopped and pulled her down, cautioning her to silence with a finger to his lips. Concealed in the cover of brush, they listened, with breath held, to the nearby sound of Waterman's footfalls as he stalked through the forest.

When the sound grew dimmer, Mike moved out and headed toward the cabin. After a short distance, he sent Ann ahead and listened to make certain they were out of earshot. The darkness and forest were his weapons. Now would be the perfect time to follow Waterman and take him out. But Ann's life depended on him, and if he failed, she'd be an easy mark for the killer.

He caught up with her and they dashed back toward the cabin. Precious moments were lost breaking the lock on the shed's door because the key was in the cabin and he dare not take that risk. He recovered the spare key for the motorcycle that he kept hidden in the shed and quickly wheeled out the bike.

Ann climbed on behind him, and Mike revved up the bike. The sound was like a gun blast in the still night. The real thing joined it when Waterman came crashing out of the forest with a blazing weapon.

Bright sparks blinked like fireflies as the bullets bounced off the metal frame of the bike, but several of the cartridges found their mark in the rear wheel. The tire popped and the bike skidded several yards then crashed to the ground sending the two riders sprawling in the dirt.

The breath was knocked out of Mike, and the pain in his arm was excruciating. He crawled over to Ann, who lay motionless nearby. She was unconscious but breathing.

Waterman strolled up casually to them and looked down at the pair. Mike was bleeding from the forehead, and Ann was knocked out. He examined her, then his mouth curved into a smirk.

"For a moment there, Agent Bishop, I thought you saved me the trouble of disposing of our lovely Miss Hamilton."

"In the name of God, Waterman, don't kill her," Mike

pleaded. He tried to reach for his gun, but his arm was broken.

"Did she ever figure out who killed Burroughs?" Waterman asked.

"She never had a clue. Still doesn't," Mike said, in the hope Waterman would spare her.

"More's the pity," Waterman said. "It's so painful to kill one so young and lovely."

"What about Charles Breton? Is he dead?"

"Had to kill him. Burroughs made a phone call to him that same morning. I couldn't take the chance he didn't tell him who was behind the sabotage."

"Was Burroughs involved with the sabotage?"

"Hell, no. I purposely asked him to investigate it knowing he was untrained and probably wouldn't get too far in his investigation."

"Obviously you were wrong."

"Yes, but because of DeVilles. He's the one who got careless."

"So DeVilles was in it with you."

"Unfortunately, I needed several accomplices. He was a close associate of Burroughs and was greedy enough to accept the offer. He was even the one who actually killed Burroughs. At my orders, of course."

"Were you behind the explosion that almost killed Amy Heather, too?"

"Another foul up by that idiot DeVilles. Thought she had dark hair, not blond, and mistook the young woman for Miss Hamilton when he blew up the ship. The man couldn't do anything right."

"Is that why you killed DeVilles?"

"The lovesick fool lost his nerve and came here to warn our little Snow White. Can you believe it? He actually was willing to cross me to try to save her! Of course, I would have had to exterminate him eventually, anyway. One can't leave loose ends lying around, can one, Bishop?''

For the first time Mike saw the glint of madness in Waterman's eyes. Somewhere along the line the man had lost his sanity.

''I suppose you're responsible for killing those two goons in Kourou,'' Waterman said.

Mike nodded. ''I don't like being shot at.''

''Naughty boy. You forced me to personally take a hand in this. Now look what it's come to. I have to tell you, you had me going in circles there for a couple days. I was afraid you were smart enough to eventually figure it all out. You're very skilled at your job, Agent Bishop. You'll be missed.''

''Then why did you even call in my team for the rescue?''

''Baker did it before I could stop him. I couldn't very well change his orders when I found out.''

''So even those guys were working for you.''

''Not really. They're infiltrators from the country that hired me to sabotage the satellite. Now, unfortunately, I have to kill you. It was never my intent. The same is true about Agent Sardino. I liked that boy.''

''You killed Tony?'' Blind with anger, Mike tried to rise.

Waterman pressed his booted foot on his broken arm. Pain shot to his head and Mike fought to hold on to consciousness.

''Actually, it was quite painful for me, but I had to. The dear boy trusted me, so he never anticipated it. I can assure you he didn't suffer.''

''But why, Waterman? Why Tony?''

''Unfortunately, he saw me in Beirut when I was negotiating the arrangements to sabotage the satellite. I knew he'd mention seeing me, and if word got back to

Baker—who would know I had no reason to be there—I'd have some serious explaining to do. Our Mr. Baker has a suspicious mind, you know.''

Waterman sighed. ''Now I'll let you decide which one of you should go first.''

''Take me out first,'' Mike said. ''Just one more question, Waterman. Why did you do it? Are you a mole?''

''No. I'm not working for any other country. The only interests I'm looking after are my own. I'm up for retirement at the end of the year.'' He snickered. ''Live out the rest of my life on that measly Agency pension? I don't think so. I deserve much more for the years I've served my country and yours. So when I got a good offer to sabotage the satellite launch, I took it.''

''What government paid you to do it?''

''I think I answered more than the one question you asked me to. Time to say goodbye, Agent Bishop.'' He raised his rifle.

''Don't even think it.''

Dave Cassidy pressed a gun to the back of Waterman's head.

''Shoot the bastard, Dave,'' Mike lashed out. ''He's the one who killed Tony.''

''Agent Cassidy! What a surprise,'' Waterman said, keeping his weapon pointed at Mike.

''It shouldn't be, sir. Did you forget we work as a team?''

''I might have known. Where's the rest of the squad?''

''Right here, sir,'' Bolen said as he and Fraser stepped out of the shadows.

Waterman laughed. ''It would appear I'm outnumbered.'' He raised his arms in surrender.

Bolen walked up and took the rifle out of Waterman's hand as Don Fraser bent down to examine Ann.

"What in hell kept you guys?" Mike said. "I was running out of questions."

"How badly are you hurt?" Cassidy asked.

"I think my arm's broken."

"You fooled me completely, Agent Bishop. I thought you were a rogue agent acting on your own," Waterman said. "Remarkable job, men. I didn't hear a sound when you moved in on me. The Agency can be proud of you. I shall recommend you all for meritorious commendations."

Mike exchanged a pitying glance with Cassidy as Dave helped him to his feet. They recognized another casualty of war. A once-brave soldier had fought one too many battles and had crossed into another world.

In the next quarter hour the fire department and sheriff's department arrived on the scene. Mike and Ann were whisked off in an ambulance to the hospital, but until the whole matter could be resolved, they would be kept in police custody.

The Agency was contacted, which in turn had to track down Jeff Baker in Disney World, where he had been vacationing with his grandchildren.

Chapter 25

By the following afternoon there was a festive attitude as Ann and her protectors congregated for lunch in the coffee shop of the motel where the squad had spent the night.

The CIA had confirmed Mike's identity and clarified the involvement of him and the squad.

Both Mike and Ann had been released from the hospital—Ann with a mild concussion and Mike with a broken arm.

Avery Waterman had made a full confession and had been turned over to the federal authorities.

The local law enforcement agency was being praised by the citizens for their expedience in solving a murder in the community.

The surrounding press was out in mass, salivating over their headlines of intrigue and murder, and making obnoxious nuisances of themselves trying to interview the players and the local man on the street.

Barney Hailey had arrived on the scene beaming happily that his beloved photographer was no longer in danger.

The Dwarf Squad was relieved that all of them had weathered another mission with nothing worse than a broken arm among them.

But…Mike and Ann were miserable.

After the initial relief that Ann no longer was in danger, Mike's thoughts had shifted to his personal problems.

His cabin was literally destroyed and would have to be razed and rebuilt. His cherished pickup—that once could do 110—had been reduced to a heap of charred metal. His Harley, which was his baby, would need a repainting and a rear wheel replacement.

Now that Mike had not been killed defending her, and her life was no longer threatened, Ann had been hit with the depression of how much she missed Brandon and the frustrating delay in obtaining custody of him. She had called him the first thing that morning only to be informed by a cold and officious voice that Brandon Burroughs was unavailable to take the call. She'd hung up the phone near tears. Now they were even keeping her from talking to him.

Ann sat in the large rounded booth surrounded by Barney and the Dwarf Squad. The men were all jovial as they ate except for Mike, who seemed to be lost in his own thoughts. Ann had no appetite and merely picked at her food. She finally put her fork aside and cradled her head in her hand.

"Do you think I can sue the British government?"

They all stopped what they were saying and looked at her.

"Annie, Waterman may be a Brit, but he was working for the American government. Although he wasn't working in behalf of the CIA when he tried to kill you."

"I'm not thinking about Waterman. I'm referring to Brandon. I have a codicil in my purse that clearly states I should receive legal custody of him. Not only have they kept us apart, but they're even preventing us from talking to each other.''

Barney winked at Mike. ''Annie girl, I'm sure quicker than you think, that will soon be a moot point.''

''Besides, Ann,'' Mike said, ''where are you going to put the kid when you do get him? You don't even have a place to live.''

''How could I when you wouldn't let me out of your sight and then hid me away up here? Not that I don't appreciate how you saved my life.''

Cassidy chuckled. ''Hear that, Mike? The little gal said she appreciates how you saved her life. Let's drink to that.'' The guys clinked their beer bottles together.

''Actually, it was a tough decision to make,'' Mike said. ''I had to choose between her or my pickup.''

''How long are you going to mourn the loss of that rattletrap?'' Ann declared.

''Bite your tongue, lady. Push the pedal to the metal on that truck and it could do—''

''A hundred and ten,'' the three-squad members shouted in unison. Which necessitated another clink of the bottles.

Despite her depression, Ann couldn't help smiling as she listened to the men. They were a remarkable team with a bond between them that was irrevocable. As proficient at their labor as the most cunning lawyer or skilled surgeon. They had to be—they put their lives on the line every time they smeared that greasepaint on their faces and walked into darkness.

They worked as a team and played as a team—and lived by the tenets of honor, duty and loyalty. Whether it was to God and country, she couldn't say, but for certain it was to each other.

And to meet and know them was worth the nightmare she'd gone through.

Her gaze shifted to Mike. She loved him so much. Was

it possible for them to have a future together, or did his membership in this unique fraternity exclude such an outside commitment? She feared the latter.

Depression crept in and took over again. Ann propped her elbows on the table, and with a woeful sigh cupped her chin in her hands.

"It's about time," Cassidy said.

Ann looked up, thinking he was talking to her, and discovered all of the men were looking at the door. She turned her head and saw what held their attention. Pete Bledsoe and Rick Williams were standing side by side in the entrance of the restaurant. They waved and then stepped apart. With a wide grin, Brandon stepped out from behind them.

"Surprise!" he shouted.

With open arms he raced across the floor. Ann was out of the booth and down on her knees when he threw himself into her arms. They hugged and kissed, and then hugged and kissed again. Then she just held him, unable to believe he was really there in her arms.

Tears streaked her cheeks when he stepped back and looked at her. "Why are you crying, Ann? Aren't you glad I'm here?"

"Oh, darling," she said, pulling him back again into her arms. "They're tears of joy, honey."

His little face glowed with happiness. "Were you surprised? We wanted to surprise you."

"You sure did, sweetheart."

"Pete and Rick brought me."

Ann sat down and lifted him onto her lap. "You mean all you guys knew about this?"

"I didn't find out until I got out of the hospital this morning," Mike said.

"Who arranged it?" she asked. "Don't tell me Waterman did."

"No," Cassidy said. "Your boss did." He gave Barney a high five.

"Thank you, Barney," she said, deeply moved. "But how did you cut through the red tape?"

"I didn't have to. A Mr. Leonard called me two days ago in an attempt to locate you. He said his office had just received a copy of the codicil Clayton Burroughs had signed making you the guardian of Brandon. Breton's secretary told him they had failed to attach it to the will and found it among a pile of loose papers in the vault. He contacted the British State Department and since you had left a document authorizing them to release Brandon to the care of Bledsoe or Williams we made reservations and they flew in today. When you return to New York, the British Embassy wants you to contact them. There are some legal papers to sign."

Ann set Brandon down beside her and then went over and hugged Barney. "Thank you, Barney. I'm so grateful to you." She went over to Rick and Pete and did the same to each of them. "I just don't know how to thank you guys enough for what you've done. I mean all of you. Dave, Kurt, Don, and you, Mike. I love all of you. I don't know how I can ever, ever thank you." Unable to control her tears, she broke down again.

Barney came over and patted her on the head. "Come on, Annie, you're making us feel bad instead of good."

She raised her head and saw Brandon watching her with sad eyes. His little chin quivering. "Please don't be sad, Ann."

She reached for him and hugged him again. "I'm fine now, sweetheart. I'm truly fine." She laughed lightly and swiped away her tears. "I don't know when I've ever felt so fine. But I have to say it one more time, then I won't mention it again. I love all of you." Then she grabbed

Brandon and put him on her lap again. "And especially this little guy."

Brandon giggled with pleasure.

As soon as they finished lunch, they all drove to Mike's cabin.

"I'm so sorry, Mike," Ann said as they viewed the destruction.

"Not your fault, Ann. It was my idea to bring you here."

While Ann and Dave packed up to leave, the fellows hauled whatever articles of value hadn't been shot up into the shed and locked it up. Then they boarded up the windows and doors and climbed into cars to head back to Milwaukee.

She and Brandon were in the back seat of Barney's rental car, and Mike climbed into his Beamer with the other five squad members. Her heart seemed to twist in her breast. For the past two weeks Mike had barely left her side and was always the one in the seat next to her. Now he was looking at her through the window of another car.

Barney rolled down the window. "Hey, we've got a spare seat in here if one of you guys wants to ride with us."

She looked hopefully at Mike, but his expression remained unchanged.

"We're cool, Barney," Kurt said, from behind the wheel of the Beamer.

Barney waved. "Okay. Hope to see you at the airport."

Ann's gaze fell on Mike again. For almost twenty-four hours they had made the most incredible love she had ever known. Had shared the most terrifying hours she had ever experienced. Now he was looking at her as if they were casual strangers.

The trip back to Milwaukee seemed to go on for hours. Brandon fell asleep huddled against her, so she stretched him out with his head in her lap.

"Is the boy asleep?" Barney asked.

"Yes."

"These past couple of weeks have been pretty hard on him, haven't they?"

"Yes, but I'll make it up to him," she said. "Everything will be okay."

"Will it be okay between you and Mike?"

"Mike? I don't understand. What are you talking about?"

"Annie, I've got eyes. A lot more than baby-sitting went on between the two of you."

"I never could fool you, could I, Barney?" she said.

"I'm sorry to hear you even think of trying. So how bad is it?"

"I'm in love with him, Mike."

"Did you tell him so?"

"No. But he's very perceptive."

"So what does he have to say on the subject?"

"I can tell you the word *love* never entered the conversation."

"The guy's got to be a fool."

"One of us is," she said with a sad smile. She leaned back and was quiet for the rest of the trip.

After a short wait at the Mitchell Field International Airport, their flight was announced for boarding.

Barney had booked them on the flight to New York and as she moved to the gate, Mike showed up to say goodbye.

"So you're heading back to New York?" he said.

She nodded. "Aren't you?"

He shook his head. "Baker canceled our leave and ordered the squad back to D.C."

"Oh, I see. Duty calls."

She felt awkward, but without a sign from him, she was too proud to broach the subject that had been on her mind the whole trip back to Milwaukee.

The announcement of the final boarding call for her flight was made and she forced a smile. "I guess I have to go now."

He kissed her lightly. "Have a safe flight."

"You, too."

He gently cupped her cheek in his palm. "I'll call you, Violet Eyes."

She smiled and hurried to the gate, paused at the door and looked back at him.

She knew he wasn't going to call.

Chapter 26

Ann heard the phone ringing as she came down the hallway. She unlocked the door as quickly as she could. Brandon skipped in ahead of her and ran to his bedroom as she rushed to the telephone. She was too late. The ringing stopped and the caller hung up without leaving a message.

Sighing, she returned the receiver to its cradle. This was the third time that week the same thing had happened.

For the past thirty days she had held on to the hope that one of these times when she answered the phone or pressed the blinking light on the answering machine she'd hear Mike's voice.

Ann went back and turned the dead bolt on the door—just as Mike had always insisted she do. Her mouth curved in a poignant smile and she could hear him scolding her whenever she had failed to do so. How long would his voice linger in her ears before she would forget the sound of it?

Wearily she kicked off her shoes and went to Brandon's

bedroom. He was already sitting in the middle of his bed watching his favorite cartoon characters on the television set that Barney had bought him.

Ann sat down beside him and slipped her arm around his shoulders. The delightful sound of his laughter lifted her spirits as he watched the antics of Ernie and Big Bird on the screen.

Shortly after, she got up, kissed the top of his towhead and went to her own room. After changing into a sweatsuit and socks, she padded in her stocking feet into the kitchen to start to prepare dinner.

While the oven preheated, she removed a chicken breast and several legs out of the refrigerator. Chicken legs were Brandon's favorite food, next to chocolate chip cookies. According to the six-year-old culinary expert, "Chicken legs, with chocolate chip cookies for dessert, was the best dinner a fella could eat."

She rolled the fowl in seasoning, then with loving care Ann placed them in a roasting pan.

She had been on a nonstop treadmill since her return from Wisconsin. Her job was on hold. Going back to work at this time was an impossibility. Thank goodness Barney understood why.

As yet, she had not found a house to her liking, and with fall approaching rapidly she had enrolled Brandon in a private school in Manhattan for the coming semester.

They had returned to Kourou and spent a busy and emotionally painful week packing up the personal items in Clayton's house and her condo. She had to decide what to retain and what to let go of—and more often than not, the decision had not been an easy one.

Clayton had been a man of refined tastes. Not only did he have many costly pieces of furniture and antiques, but he also had an expensive art collection that she felt should be properly crated and stored until Brandon was old enough to make a decision of what he wished to do with it.

Working with a well renowned consultant, she shipped most of the art collection to an art museum in New York where it would be cared for and preserved more properly than if it was left stored in a warehouse for years.

As for the retained items, some had to be marked for shipment to her rental apartment in New York, and others marked for shipment to a storage facility until she had a permanent residence.

But so many items such as a grand piano and other expensive pieces of furniture and household items would have to be disposed of at an auction. Ann turned such arrangements, as well as the sale of the two residences, over to a real estate broker.

She had decided to forego the sale of the villa Clayton had willed her until a later date. It could remain in the care of Guillaume and Marie Sellier until all of the more pressing business in Kourou was completed.

Then there'd been the issue of Brandon. In the past week she had interviewed over twenty nannies. Either they did not have green cards or she wasn't impressed with them. She would not release him to the care of someone she wasn't totally comfortable with. She had even called Sarah Millen at the British Embassy in D.C. Brandon had liked the older woman and Ann thought she would make an ideal nanny for him. However, the woman was returning to England to be with her daughter who was having a baby.

And through it all, try as she might, she couldn't shake the thought of Mike out of her mind—or heart.

Lord knows you tried often enough, Ann.

It had been a month since he kissed her goodbye at the

airport. She had not heard from him since. No phone call.
No letter. Not even an e-mail.

Did you really expect he would?

Of course, there was the possibility that he didn't know
her telephone number, much less her e-mail address.

Right, Ann. Especially for a man who works for an intelligence agency.

Maybe it was for the best. They were so different. She
was no longer that young girl who came out of college
expecting to conquer the world. At this stage in her life
her heart was no longer on a career; it had become simply
a means of support. She was ready for a less hectic life
where she could devote her time to children and a home.
Not stress herself out over some pampered model delaying
a shoot.

But, of course, Mike had been a major player in that
scenario. Having him near, hearing his laughter. The scent
of him. The strength of his touch. Being able just to reach
out and touch him. Tolerating the impatience of his bad
moods and the tenderness of his teasing ones. Loving him.
Being loved.

That had all been part of the scenario, too. The peace
of mind in knowing that every night he'd come through
the door, and lie safely beside her through the night. Not
having her stomach tied into knots knowing the danger he
faced every time he went on an assignment to some name-
less country to confront a faceless enemy.

How long are you going to go on kidding yourself, Ann?
You'd take him any way you could get him.

"Shut up," she declared, and flung down the knife she'd
been using to chop up the vegetables for a salad.

For weeks she had been waging this internal battle. Trying to convince herself she could find a life so much better

without Mike Bishop. But her nefarious alter ego always won the debate with the same argument.

You can learn to live with the risks he takes, Ann. You love him too much to be without him. Think of all the other women whose men are in the military, law enforcement, the fire department. Men who work undercover dealing with drug dealers and the other scum of the world. There are hundreds of thousands of them out there risking their lives every day. And for every one, somewhere there's a woman who loves him. Come on, girl. Get real. Isn't a little part of Mike's life better than none at all?

Ann snorted. "What's the difference, anyway? Apparently Mike has settled the issue for me." She picked up the knife and resumed chopping the vegetables.

She had even developed the film and sent him the pictures and negatives she'd shot of him and the other squad members, including those beefcake ones she had taken of him in his cabin. She had kept the three he'd taken of her, and one other photo: a candid shot she'd taken in New York when she'd caught his grin on film. That endearing grin that transferred warrior to boy and never failed to tug at her heartstrings.

Maybe it was a mistake not to send him those nude photos of myself, she thought. They might have tempted him enough to pick up the telephone.

"Oh, go away." she said to the thought, and shoved the pan of chicken into the oven.

As they ate dinner Ann listened with delight as Brandon went on about the worth of a chicken. "It's got to be just about the best animal there is."

"Honey, a chicken is a fowl, not a mammal."

"It tastes 'bout the best of any meat."

"But many, many people don't eat meat, Brandon."

"Chickens make eggs, too." He raised his hands apart

and leaned his head toward her, his eyes wide with intensity. "You see, Ann, that's what I mean about chickens. If a kid doesn't like meat, he could always eat eggs." His face curled into a serious frown. "Yep, a chicken's gotta be 'bout the best animal...I mean fowl...there is."

Ann's heart overflowed with love. She had all she could do to keep from snatching him up and hugging him. She forced back a smile and attempted to look serious.

"But Brandon, consider a cow. It offers beef. That makes it very worthy."

"Don't like beef as much as chicken."

"But a cow gives milk, too, dear. And not only that, its size is so much larger than a chicken's that it produces a greater source of beef and milk."

His mouth puckered, and a serious frown creased his brow. The little munchkin was not about to go down without a fight.

"So what, Ann. You always said good things come in small packages."

"That's true. You're a small package."

"What about Mike, Ann? He's big. Don't you think he's a good thing?"

"Sweetheart, how did this conversation get from chickens and cows to Mike Bishop?" She stood up quickly and began to clear the table. "And don't lick your fingers, Brandon. Use your napkin."

Later she drew his bath, and while he bathed she did the dinner dishes. Then she tucked him in bed. While she was reading to him, there was a knock at the door.

"Now, who could that be?" she said.

Brandon jumped out of bed. "Bet it's Barney," he said hopefully. "He told me on the telephone that he's got a big surprise for me."

When Ann opened the door, her breath caught in her throat, and she stared speechlessly at Mike Bishop.

"I see you're still opening doors without checking who's on the other side."

The same Mike—as crotchety as ever about security. They hadn't seen or spoken to each other for four weeks, and the first words out of his mouth were a reprimand.

Ann wanted to shout with joy, but she was too breathless to make a sound. She felt deliriously, dizzyingly, delightfully, and all those other *D* adverbs—or were they adjectives—overcome with happiness.

God was in his Heaven again and Mike Bishop was back in charge down here.

"May I come in, Ann?"

She nodded and managed to step aside, even though her legs were trembling so badly they could hardly support her.

"Mike!" Brandon streaked across the floor.

"How you doing, pal?"

The two of them high fived, then Brandon jumped up into his arms. Maybe she should have tried that. It might be better than just standing and gaping at him. But, oh, he looked so good.

Mike put Brandon back down on his feet, and then handed him the box he'd struggled not to drop when Brandon jumped up on him. "I brought you a little present." He shifted his gaze back to her. "It's some kind of electronic robot. Batteries not included."

"Wow! Can I open it now?"

"Sweetheart, take it into your room, and we'll get some batteries for it tomorrow. It's past your bedtime now, and Mike and I have some business to discuss."

He wasn't happy about it, but started to leave, clutching

the box. Then he suddenly stopped and turned around. "Mike, which do you like the best? Chicken or beef?"

Ann had been around Mike long enough to know the man would eat a steak a day if given the choice. But she held a great regard for that sixth-sense perception of his.

For the length of a drawn breath, he hesitated. "Chicken, pal."

Brandon flashed a wide grin. "Good night, Mike, and thanks for the robot."

"I'll be back shortly," Ann said. "I just have to tuck him in." They were the first words she spoke directly to him since he arrived.

Chapter 27

Mike moved to the bedroom door and peeked in. Brandon was sitting up in bed with his hands folded in prayer.

"Please, God, bless Ann and Mike and Barney and Pete and Rick and Dave and Don and Kurt and Jimmy the doorman and Patty the switchboard operator. She's the one with the red hair who always gives me a piece of candy when she sees me."

Ann was kneeling at his bedside with her head bowed. Mike's hungry gaze devoured the beautiful lines of her profile as the youngster continued.

"And bless Jeremy over in England, and Mrs. Millen and her daughter and little baby." He frowned in deep concentration. "Do you think I should bless Mrs. Hubbard, Ann? I didn't like her very much but she really wasn't mean to me."

"Well then, I think you should, sweetheart," Ann said softly.

"And bless Mrs. Hubbard…and…" He yawned and his eyes began to droop.

"Sweetheart, why don't you just ask God to bless all the children and anyone who loves Him or needs His help?"

Brandon nodded. "And please bless all the children in the whole world, and all who love You and need Your help. And take care of Grandfather and Daddy and Mommy in Heaven with You. And, God, thank you for sending me a new mommy. And thank you for the robot, too. We're going to get batteries for it tomorrow. Amen." He flopped his head down on the pillow.

Mike grinned. What a kid. He moved away and studied the pictures on the wall. Ann had the place looking real homey in the short time she'd been there.

He couldn't remember a time he felt so nervous. He had to talk himself into staying calm before every mission, but coming here tonight had been the hardest decision he'd ever made.

Mike sat down and began to nervously drum his fingers against the arm of the chair. The delay was working on nerves that were half-gone to begin with. He leaped to his feet when Ann came out of the bedroom and carefully closed the door.

"He's asleep already. We've been on the go all day, so he was really tuckered out. Can I get you something to drink? I'm afraid I don't have any beer though. How about a cup of coffee?"

"No, thanks. If I drink any more coffee, I can probably fly back to D.C. on my own steam." A straight shot of hundred proof would help, but he wasn't about to ask for booze since he already was on a caffeine high.

"I don't even have any wine to offer you," she said.

"No problem, Ann. I'm cool."

She seated herself on the couch, so he sat back down in the chair.

"Well, this is a surprise, Mike. What brings you to New York?"

The situation was becoming more ludicrous by the minute. They were acting and talking like two stiff-necks in a Victorian novel. He'd had enough of the game. He would say what he came to say. Make his apology and then get the hell out of there if she told him to.

At least, that was his intention until he opened his mouth. "I got the pictures. Thank you. But where in hell are the three I took of you?"

Her eyes widened in disgust. "*That's* the reason you came here!" She jumped to her feet. "You perverted bastard! Get out of here."

He was on her at once. Grasping her by the shoulders, he looked into the withering scorn of her glare. "Ann, that's not what I meant to say."

"No doubt. A Freudian slip, Bishop? You've got to be really sick to come all this way for three damn pictures. And I must be as depraved as you to have gone along with it."

"You've got it all wrong Ann. I came to apologize. I know I have no right to show up here on your doorstep, and I tried to stay away, but I couldn't any longer."

He released his hold on her, and she stepped away shaking her head in bewilderment.

"Apologize for what?"

"I almost got you killed."

"Let it go, Mike! We've been through that before. I don't blame you for what happened. And if it weren't for you, Brandon and I could both be dead. So stop beating a dead horse. I'm not looking at you through the eyes of the Agency. You may have slipped a little in duty ethics in their eyes, but in mine you protected Brandon and me, and saved our lives. Mission accomplished."

"I don't see it that way."

Frustrated, she spun to face him. "For God's sake, how do you people reason? What do you want me to say, Mike? You were negligent, so I can't forgive you even though you saved my life. Sounds ridiculous, doesn't it? What happened in your cabin was predictable. We were two adults sexually attracted to each other, and the outcome was inevitable. And when we said goodbye in Milwaukee, I knew it was over and you never intended to call me."

"That's not true. I've called you a dozen times, but I hung up before you answered."

Her anger had cooled, but her confusion was obvious. "I don't think you would lie to me, Mike, but I don't understand all of this. What is your real motive for coming here? To apologize? Is that it? Somehow ease your conscience? It would have been a lot easier and less embarrassing for both of us if you had given me your slam-bam, thank you, ma'am message by telephone. I even have an answering machine you could have left it on. Or an e-mail or letter would have enabled you not to even say it aloud. Wouldn't that have been less personal?"

All the fight drained out of him. He figured she'd be angry, but he hadn't anticipated such bitterness from her. His heart felt squeezed in his chest and ached like hell.

"You don't take prisoners, do you?"

She turned away. "Like you do?" she said sarcastically.

He walked up behind her and put his hands on her shoulders. "I never intended to hurt you, Ann. That night in the cabin I knew we both were out of control, but I figured we were old enough to know what we were doing and could work it out in the end. That was a class-A blunder on my part. I knew we were already in too deep before we even had sex. That this wouldn't be just another one-night stand. This time it was different. But I let it happen, anyway."

She turned and faced him. His knees almost buckled at

the sight of her eyes. Misty with tears, they were velvet pools that lured his soul into their depths.

"Why was this time different, Mike?"

"When I made love to you, Ann, I defied every principle I'd lived by since I joined the Agency—I let my personal needs affect my duty. You once accused me of putting my professional reputation ahead of anything else in my life. You were right. That and the men in the squad had been my only focus until you entered my life. Ann, I would have thrown it all up for grabs if there'd been somewhere I could have taken you and known you'd be safe forever. Instead, I had to try to hold on to the only structure I knew and could rely on—training, objectivity and discipline. And when I realized I was in love with you, all three went down the tube."

Her quick gasp was as much of a turn-on to him as the glow in her luminous eyes. "Did you say you're in love with me?"

"Did you actually believe I thought you were just another woman I had sex with? Another one-night stand? How could you think that night didn't mean anything to me? Of course I'm in love with you, Ann. Why do you think I've been making an ass of myself?"

"Oh, Mike!" She threw her arms around his neck, and he pulled her tighter and kissed her.

His body erupted with sensation. Just like their first time. Instant. Hot. Her soft, rounded curves molded to the hardened angles of his, and their mouths and tongues worked in tandem.

Lord how he needed her. Had thought of nothing else for a month except how she felt in his arms. How she tasted. How she smelled. Her smile. Her walk. The sound of her voice.

He was so hard and ready he hoped he could make it

to her bedroom. He had to break the kiss or he'd end up flying solo without her.

"Why? Why didn't you say so sooner?" she asked breathlessly.

Thirty days was too long for any red-blooded man to be apart from the woman he loved. Answers could come later. Right now time was critical.

Mike swept her up in his arms. "So which door is yours?"

"I'd better get out of here and let you get some sleep," Mike said later.

"No, don't leave, Mike. Not yet."

"What if Brandon wakes up? I don't want him to find us in bed together. I never liked the idea of single mothers with live-in boyfriends."

"You're such a fraud, Bishop. Despite all that cocky womanizing you profess to indulge in, you're an old-fashioned moralist at heart," she said contentedly, and laid her head on his chest. "But I agree. We won't make love when he's around."

"I have to go back to D.C. tomorrow anyway."

"There's no reason why you can't stay tonight. I'll put you up on the coach. Brandon won't think anything of it. He's used to having you around.

"I wish you could stay longer though." Ann raised her head and tried to appear casual. "Has your arm healed well enough for you to get back on a mission?"

He wove his fingers through her hair. "I've always been a quick healer."

"That's good," she said. She laid her head back down on his chest. "How long do you expect to be gone?"

"I should be able to come back next weekend and we can get married."

She popped up her head again. "Are you proposing?"

"Or better yet. Why don't you and Brandon come back to D.C. with me tomorrow and we can find a place for all of us?"

Things were moving too swiftly to keep up with them. She had to slow down and start sorting them out.

"Mike, slow up. Let's not rush into anything."

He misread her intent. "I guess I did take it for granted you'd feel the same way about us as I do. I remember you did say once that you'd never marry a man who lived on the edge like I did—"

"I wasn't in love with you at the time. That's all changed. Now I can't think of being without you. What I meant is we shouldn't rush into marriage. I know with your job you have to stay focused when you're on a mission. Look what happened in your cabin. And it would be worse with a wife and family hanging around your neck. So you don't have to marry me, Mike. I'll settle for any time we can have together. Wife or mistress."

He cupped her cheek in his hand. "You'd do that for me, Violet Eyes?"

She kissed his palm. "I love you, Mike." She settled back down on his chest again. His arm tightened around her.

"Do you think we can make it with love, Ann?" he asked solemnly. "Lord knows I'm a hell of a prospect for a husband, sweetheart, but if love is any help, I have enough to last us a lifetime."

"That's all I'll ever ask of you, my love."

"This is a good time to tell you that I've changed some of my thinking, too. In the past month I came to the conclusion that a life of intrigue and danger could never stack up to spending the rest of my life with you and Brandon. So I made a career change."

She sat up, distressed. "Mike, don't tell me you left the CIA?"

"No, but with Waterman gone the Agency was looking for someone to fill his place. They offered it to me and I accepted. Dave's been moved up to squad leader."

"Mike, you did that because of me. I won't let you do it. You'll be miserable behind a desk."

"Misery was these past thirty days without you. I can't go through that again."

"It wasn't exactly a holiday for me, either," she said.

"I'm sorry, honey," he said. "I knew you hated the work I was in, and thought I'd be doing you a favor by getting out of your life. But I couldn't stay away any longer."

"Thank God," she said, burying her head against his chest.

"For a long time I've wanted something more in life than what I had, Ann. I found out what it was when you came into my life." He pulled her back down and kissed her. "Baby, no job is worth giving up the chance to come home to you every night," he said tenderly.

"Any more than me thinking I could put a desire for peace of mind ahead of who or what my heart desires," she said. "I guess we both learned a lesson about love. But are you sure this is what you want, Mike? You're the one making the sacrifice, so whenever you feel you want to go back to the excitement of your other life, I'll understand."

And she meant it, too, because nothing could mar her happiness now. She had Mike and Brandon. "So it looks like Brandon and I will be moving to Washington?"

"There or Virginia. Do you mind, Ann? That's where my job is. Barney told me you've cleared up all the legal matters concerning Brandon."

"Yes." She looked up at him, her eyes glowing with happiness. "I'm legally his mother now. The adoption papers were signed last week." With a delightful chuckle she added. ''And are you aware I have a very wealthy son? The extent of Clayton's wealth even astounded me. I had it all transferred into a trust until Brandon's twenty-five. When he's about eighteen, he'll probably want to strangle me for not allowing him to get his hands on it sooner.''

''You did right, Ann.''

Her sigh of contentment belied her words. ''Here I go. Packing up again. It's going to be hard to tell Barney I won't be coming back to work.''

''The first crisis already.'' He chuckled. ''Honey, you don't have to give up your career if you don't want to. Barney said he can set up shoots in D.C. for you.''

She frowned. ''You spoke to Barney about this?''

Mike looked uncomfortable. ''A little bit.'' He got out of bed hastily and pulled on his jeans. ''Where do you keep the sheets? I'll shift to the couch.''

''When?'' She climbed out of bed and put on her robe.

''Now. I'll get out of here so you can get some sleep.''

''You know that's not what I mean. *When* did you speak to Barney?''

''Earlier tonight. Before I came here.''

''Why did you go to see Barney?'' She was feeling more suspicious by the moment.

''Barney and I have a business arrangement.''

''What kind of business arrangement? Mike Bishop, what aren't you telling me?''

''I made a deal with him. He's agreed to letting you do some shoots in D.C., and—''

''And what did you agree to do in return?'' she asked.

''Sign off on those pictures you took of me.''

''You showed him those pictures! Oh, Mike, what will this do to your career if your face is splashed all over billboards and magazines?''

''Kind of sealed my fate. Looks like I'll be cushioned

behind that desk for a long time. Probably could never go back to field work even if I wanted to.''

Then he broke out into a wide grin, picked her up and swung her around. ''Guess that means you're stuck with me for life, Violet Eyes.''

Chapter 28

The following week in a private ceremony in Washington, D.C., attended only by Barney Hailey, Jeff Baker and the five members of the Dwarf Squad, Ann and Mike pledged their marriage vows as Brandon stood between them holding a hand of each of them.

When the preacher pronounced them man and wife, the youngster beamed with happiness as he looked up and saw the new father kiss the new mother God had sent him.

Across the room, arms folded across his barrel chest, Jeff Baker had listened and watched the whole proceedings with a disgruntled frown on his beefy countenance. He finally shook his head and grumbled, ''It's not gonna work.''

''With your permission, sir, I disagree,'' Dave Cassidy said. ''Mike and Ann are made for each other.''

''Just the same, the whole thing sucks. I've lost one of the best agents I've ever had in the field. No offense, Agent Cassidy. I'm sure you'll be as effective a squad leader as Bishop will be as my deputy secretary,'' Baker said.

"Well then, if you're sincere, sir, why do you have these reservations?"

"Because this isn't how the story ended. Snow White is supposed to marry Prince Charming. Not Grumpy."

Baker scratched his head and, perplexed, the gruff, seasoned ex-Marine, heralded secretary general of RATCOM—the Rescue and Anti-Terrorist Division of the CIA—glanced at the Dwarf Squad's new leader standing beside him.

"And I'm Prince Charming—ain't I?"

*   *   *   *   *

From the *USA TODAY* bestselling author of
Whiskey Island, Emilie Richards continues
her unforgettable tale of star-crossed lovers,
murder and three sisters who discover a hidden
legacy that will lead them home at last to Ireland.

"Emilie Richards presents us with a powerfully told story that
will linger in the heart long after the final page."
—*Book Page*

EMILIE
RICHARDS

THE
PARTING
GLASS

*Available in
June 2004
wherever
paperbacks
are sold.*

MIRA®

COMING NEXT MONTH

SIMCNM0604